WH SOMEONE ELSE?

ISANGELIC REYES

Prologue

"Dad, what the hell is this?" Summer gasped, gaping down the hall at the two people in a lip lock.

"Summer, honey, it's not what it looks like," her father said, nervously trying to hide the young lady with his body.

"What do you mean it's not what it looks like. What am I, five?" she slammed the front door behind her and began walking toward them.

"Just give me as second to explain —"

"Explain what?" Summer pushed her dad away in an attempt to get a good look at the lady's face. "Seriously, dad! You are cheating on mom with your secretary — of all people?"

"Can you please go. I need to talk to my daughter," her dad said under his breath to the woman.

1

"Where is she going?" Summer turned to pursue the escaping female, but her dad grabbed her by the arm and dragged her to the living room.

"Sit." Her dad clenched his jaw and pointed with his finger at the green sofa behind her.

Summer obeyed without saying another word or even looking at him. Crossing her arms, she focused on the brown coffee table in front of her. Even though her dad had started to give his speech, she couldn't register anything he was saying. Anger was causing her heart to beat incredibly fast. Then it began to ache from all the hatred entering its walls. Tears were streaming down her face, but they never made it to her neck since she kept furiously wiping her face, hating the thought of crying in front of her father. Instead of trying to listen to words that were no more than a muffled sound in her ears, Summer turned to the questions spinning around in her head. *How long has he been lying to our family? What kind of person could do such a thing? Have I never really known who he is?* The sight of her dad kissing a woman who was not her mom had pushed out any good memories she'd ever had of him. *Was he so unhappy with his family? Or did he just get bored and tired of being a husband — and of being a father to Winter and me?*

"Summer, can you please say something?" Her dad was sitting on the chair across from his daughter, looking intently at her as he fidgeted his fingers.

"I am going to tell mom," Summer stood up, ran back to the hall, and locked herself in her bedroom.

As soon as she was inside, her dad began to bang on the door, begging her to open it. "Please, let me talk to your mom first, Summer. Just think about how things are going to change if you tell her. Just give me another chance, and I promise I won't let it happen again."

"If you cared so much about mom, you would not have done this in the first place," Summer screamed from the other side of the door. "I hope I never have to see your face again."

"Summer, please —"

3

"Go! Just leave me alone, for once." Summer fell to her knees and began to take deep breaths. "I hate you. I hate you so much, Dad. I freakin' hate you."

Summer heard her father's steps retreating down the hall. At the sound of the front door slamming, she let out a loud cry.

"Why, why, why?" Summer kept screaming until her sobs became quieter.

Thirty minutes before, life had been completely normal. *If only I had stayed at the pep rally instead of coming home early. If only... oh, Winter! She can't find out about this. It would destroy her.* Soon the pep rally would be over, and Winter would be on her way home with her friends. Summer needed to think of something fast to make her stay away from the house for the rest of the day.

Suddenly Summer was startled at the sound of the ringtone from her phone. It was Winter.

"No, no, no! What am I supposed to say?" Summer stood up and started to walk back and forth while biting her finger nails.

Summer considered whether or not to tell her little sister about their dad. Would she get in trouble for telling her?

After Summer answered the call, she slowly raised the phone to her right ear. "Hello," she said, softly and carefully.

"Hey, Summer. Can you tell mom and dad that I'm staying at Beth's house tonight to work on a science project? Neither of them is picking up the phone. Thank you, sis. You're the best. Bye!" Click. That was it.

The call was certainly easier than what Summer had expected. All of that worry, all it had required from her was a "hello." Hopefully with Winter away for the night, their parents could figure things out and her sister would never have to know about it. The only thing Summer had to do was get her mother safely to the house and then tell her what she had seen.

~

Five hours had passed. Summer was sitting on the same green sofa in the living room waiting for her mother to get home from work before her dad decided to show back up. The moment she heard the rattle of the keys; Summer's hands began to shake, and her heart sank to her stomach.

"Please let it be mom," she said under her breath.

The moment Summer saw her mother enter the house, she leaped up from the sofa and ran to hug her.

"Hold on! Since when do you greet me like this?" Summer's mom said, returning the hug. "Is something wrong?"

Summer began to cry on her mother's shoulder while still holding onto her tightly.

"Oh, honey, what's wrong? Did something happen?" She grabbed her daughter's face and began wiping the tears off her red cheeks.

"It's dad!" she cried.

"What do you mean? Did something happen to your dad? Where is he?" her mom began to look around, but the house was as still as a clear-blue sky.

6

"Mom, I caught him kissing his secretary in our house, and he didn't even apologize. Do you know what he said? He told me not to tell you about it and that he won't do it again! I hate him, mom. I hate him so much, and I'm sorry that you have to hate him, now. I am so sorry, mom." Summer kept crying, and her mother held her tighter for a couple of seconds — until they heard footsteps coming from behind them.

They turned around to find that the man they were talking about had arrived at the scene.

"Honey, can you give us a moment?" Summer's mother gently requested.

When Summer reached her room, she turned around to see her mother slapping her father's face. The moment Summer gasped, her parents' heads turned quickly toward her direction. Summer, scared, went into her bedroom, locking the door behind her. She threw herself on her bed and lay there for over an hour, listening to arguments, slamming doors, and screams. She knew her mother's pain was different than what she was feeling. Summer had never even been in love. Her mother, on the other hand, had loved her dad for the past two decades. She had dedicated her whole life to him. *And this is what she gets,* Summer fumed — *a cheater, a liar, a hypocrite?*

Sooner or later Winter would know that something was amiss. How could she miss it when all of their dad's items were gone from the house? How were her parents going to tell their other daughter that they had decided to be permanently separated? *What kind of story or lie will those two come up with?* she asked herself.

It took another two more hours before Summer was finally able to get out of her room and see all of the changes done to the house. Broken picture frames were strewn everywhere. Socks and shirts were stacked in random heaps on the kitchen floor near the black trashcan. Summer checked to assure herself that her dad was long gone. She fervently hoped that she had seen him for the last time; she never wanted to have someone like him in her life again.

As her mind flooded with memories of her dad, she began to laugh sarcastically at the way he used to brag about how good-looking he was in his teens and how he was able to get every girl he desired. It seemed that he'd never really changed at all. Summer was slowing coming to realize that her father was not the person she thought he was. *One thing for sure: he never loved me. The first man to love a girl should be her father, but if dad really loved me, he wouldn't have thrown us all away.*

Summer realized how drastically her mom's life was going to change after that day. As she looked at her mom from the bedroom door, all she could think of was that she never wanted to end up like her — heartbroken.

Two years later, and Winter was still clueless about the reason for her parents' divorce. As a result, she kept in contact with their dad — even after he started a new family with the same woman of the kissing incident. For her part, Summer had kept her vow not to fall in love. She stayed away from boys because of the lingering anxiety and

9

fear that all males were like her dad — someone who could never be trusted. She knew that wasn't true since she had met some classmates that were sweet to her, but she had also dealt with cocky football players who thought they could get away with anything.

On the other hand, since Winter had no clue about what their dad was capable of, she hadn't been staying away from boys. In fact, she liked those cocky kinds of guys and that's why she was always getting her heart broken. The kids at high school found it hard to believe that the two were sisters because of how different they were from one another. Summer was quiet and smart, but she was not outgoing and also kind of boring. As a result, she was always alone. Her sister, Winter, on the other hand was popular and funny and always surrounded by people. Everybody seemed to like Winter while no one seemed to even know Summer existed.

In those post-divorce days, Winter didn't seem to care much about the guys she dated. Summer couldn't even recall the last time she saw her sister cry after a breakup. It saddened Summer to see the spark from her sister's green eyes dim little by little with each heartbreak. But somehow, Winter still managed to put on a big, bright smile as if nothing bad were going on in her love life. *If only Winter would slow down a little and enjoy her high school years without all the boy drama!* Everywhere she went, she seemed determined to attach herself to someone until the relationship fizzled out. *If Winter hasn't learned from her mistakes after all these years, Summer had begun to think, she probably never will.*

True, Summer hadn't heard about a new guy for over two months, which was unusual and also pretty impressive. She wondered if Winter had been keeping things from her or if she was just too busy to mention her new guy. With Winter's summer-camp schedule and Summer's working hours, the sisters had barely seen each other or spent time together all summer. Sometimes, Summer wished things hadn't changed from when they were younger, but every year, life seemed to get busier and busier. *Maybe before school begins next week, we can hang out a little and talk.*

Winter was an hour late. Usually she would send a text message when she was running late, but that day, Summer didn't get a single text or call. She didn't want to bother her sister just in case she was still driving or at an important meeting or something. *Who am I kidding?* Summer thought. *No way would Winter just leave her high and dry. So, where is she and why hasn't she called?*

After another hour, Summer decided to give her sister a call. She didn't want to be the annoying, overprotective sister; but she was worried sick, and her anxiety was getting out of control. A few seconds later, Winter slammed into the house and stomped into her bedroom. The only times Summer had ever seen Winter do that were when she was a spoiled little brat and didn't get what she wanted and then, last year, after Mark cheated on her.

As Summer came into Winter's room and sat next to her, she began to think of things to say. She couldn't even tell what Winter was feeling since her face was covered by her bright-pink stuffed animal. Summer felt as if she was walking on eggshells. She had always been

12

afraid of saying the wrong thing at the worst time, and right then, she had no clue about what was going on.

"Winter, do you want to talk about it?"

"I think I just ruined the only true relationship I have ever had in my life!" she groaned as she moved the stuffed animal away. Her face was strawberry red and her eyes the darkest green Summer has ever seen. This color change used to happen when they were kids but only when Winter had been crying for a while.

"What do you mean? I thought you weren't dating anyone at the moment."

"I am. Well, I was. I was dating this sweet, cute guy from camp, and I really was going to tell you about him. I just forgot to. I'm sorry." Tears began to run down Winter's cheeks and then all the way to her neck. There, they began to soak her straight hair, making its strands stick to her skin like a magnet.

"What did you do, Winter?" Summer asked, knowing that she was being too direct, but needing to catch Winter before she started to change to another subject so that she would not have to talk to her about the breakup. Winter was uncomfortable, and Summer couldn't understand why. They were sisters. They knew everything about each other. What could she have done to be the one breaking someone's heart?

"He caught me cheating on him."

Chapter 1

My name is Summer. That alone should be enough for me to love that season, but I have much better reasons for it to be my favorite time of year.

Summer weather is just perfect. It might be a little bit too hot sometimes, but that is nothing a good swim at the beach can't fix. During the summer, you can have endless days full of sunshine and so many fun adventures. Summer sunsets at the beach are to die for as well — even if you don't have anyone to watch them with. I wish we could keep the same season all year the way some places do. I would love to have been born on a tropical island rather than the dreary coast of South Carolina. But instead, I am getting ready to buy more outfits for the extremely cold weather that is coming in a couple of months. And some people are looking forward to it! (How can someone think it's so much fun to go on a walk when it's fifty degrees outside?)

I guess I'm just a little self-absorbed — or at least immature — for thinking that everyone's favorite season is the same as mine. I still haven't met anybody who loves summertime as much as I do. One day I wanted to be able to share that connection with another person so that we could also share crazy summertime adventures. Up to that time, all I had was myself and my little sister, Winter, at least sometimes. I'd barely spent any time with her that summer because she was always busy with something, and whenever she wasn't, she was too tired to go out with me. So basically, I can say that it had been the loneliest summer I'd had since my dad moved away to Texas with his new girlfriend and step-kids. I hated him for doing that to us. Winter hadn't been the same since he'd moved over 1,000 miles away from our home.

At this point, I hadn't talked to my dad for a year since I was still angry at him for hurting my mother. *Maybe, one day,* I thought, *I will pick up the phone when he calls, but right now, I doubt I will ever forgive him for abandoning us so easily.* Why did I think for a second that he was going to fight for mom? *No wonder I hate this time of the year.* My dad and my sister used to love autumn so much that every single weekend they would do something together without me because they knew how much I disliked the decorations and Halloween. I remember sitting inside the house, watching them from the living room window and wondering why they never tried to include me in any of their activities. Probably I would have said no to them, but some days I wanted to be included.

But summer was different. In that season, my dad used to spend time with me alone because my sister hated the beach and couldn't swim. Maybe he focused on spending more time with Winter during the fall to make sure she didn't feel left out. I find it weird that he didn't make us spend time with each other instead of just assuming one of us didn't want to go out or participate. No kid wants to spend the day in her bedroom while her sibling is having fun outside. Somehow, this was my parents' bizarre way to spend more quality time with their two daughters. Dad would play with one of his daughters while mom would attend to the other.

My sister and I agreed that mother was the boring, strict parent; that is why I hated looking exactly like her — with her curly black hair and dark brown eyes. I hated that sometimes I acted like her as well. I wish I was my own person without mirroring either of my parents, whom I didn't look up to anymore. It was so hard to have a mind of my own when I had my parents' voices in the back of my head telling me what to do all the time. I just wanted to stop being so influenced by them. I wanted to open up my interests and maybe try to learn to like autumn and cold weather like Winter did. I wanted to be able to enjoy the things she liked to do, to spend more time with her before life got ahead of us and we were not living together anymore.

That is the only reason I agreed to go shopping with her that day. I disliked shopping as much as I disliked hot coffee, but if I wanted to overcome all the ways my parents had influenced my personality, I needed to make an effort to actually get out of my comfort zone.

"Earth to Summer. Do you think I should get the brown sweatshirt or the orange one?" asked my dear sister (who was, by the way, two years younger than I but still acted as if she was the eldest). Since I didn't react right away to her question, she proceeded to wave her small hands in front of my face to get my attention.

If only I could have been as enthusiastic as she was about cold weather, I probably would have been looking around for warm clothing instead of being lost in my thoughts on how to be a good sister. I just wished she didn't have such an expensive taste in clothing. *Why is everything in this store more than fifty dollars?* I thought. I might have agreed to go shopping for new school clothes with her, but I refused to go broke in the process. How could I be enthusiastic about shopping when everything in that store was too expensive for me? But of course, Winter didn't have any worries about the price of a sweatshirt. All the money my sister received from our dad every week she spent on designer clothes. I wish I'd had the opportunity to do that just two years ago when I was her age.

"You know, if you didn't want to come shopping, you didn't have to bother," she said with an attitude while chewing a piece of bubblegum.

"Of course I wanted to come. I'm just a bit stressed. That's all," I said to try to hide my discomfort at being in this particular clothing store. "I think the brown one will look a whole lot better since it makes your blue eyes pop out more. Plus, don't you already have an orange sweatshirt?" I realized that only because just the night before, I had been looking on my phone through Winter's Instagram photos to try to get an idea of the activities she usually liked to do during the fall. I hoped she didn't think that I was stalking her, but then again, she never put much effort into connecting the dots in situations like that.

"Mmm… You're right. Thank you, Sis. I knew it was a great idea for you to come with me. You have a good eye for fashion and a pretty good memory." She returned the orange sweatshirt to its rack and walked past me to look at a pair of blue jeans across the shop. She seemed really determined to find the perfect outfits for that week. *Maybe she should be the one going to fashion school and not me,* I thought.

"If you say so." I began to walk in another direction, closer to the door, so that I could start signaling her that after spending an hour in that store, I wanted to leave. It was mostly because I was bored to death, but I was also really hungry.

I wondered if she would ever experience what I was going through at that time. Already I was feeling stressed about my senior year of high school with all its pressure of making good grades, and we hadn't even started school yet. Winter's grades had been getting worse and worse every year, and neither of my parents seemed to care about it. I guess that is the kind of treatment the youngest child gets. It's just not fair. Dad and mom always got mad at me if I failed a test. They wanted me to be the smart one. With all the studying every night, I barely got a chance to make very many friends growing up.

Maybe my parents saw how boring my life had become and decided to go a little easier on my sister. But since the divorce they just didn't seem to care deeply about her well-being anymore. I hadn't heard them giving her romantic advice — or any kind of life advice, for that matter. They just let her make mistake after mistake, probably just hoping that she would make it through and at least learn from the mistakes.

At times, the way Winter treated our mother wasn't fair either. She hadn't ever said it, but she blamed our mother for our parents' separation even though it was clear on paper that it was my dad who cheated and did not care to fight for their marriage. Ever since our dad left us, our mom had been managing all of the bills, and I had been helping out with the household chores. Winter never did anything to help out because she thought that it wasn't her responsibility. What infuriated me most was that she didn't seem to care about anything or anyone but herself. Still, she was my sister, and I cared about her as much as I cared about myself.

That day, I really wanted us to enjoy spending time together. I didn't anticipate how much my enjoyment would decrease with not having money to spend. Before our parents' divorce, I didn't really give much thought to how I was going to pay for college. But at that point, my only hope was to get an academic scholarship that would at least help me with my first year of college. If life really was as easy as Winter liked to think, I would make the stupid decision of becoming a fashion designer even though I hated clothes with all my heart. I didn't think she would ever notice how unrealistic her dreams for me were, especially when I had no interest in becoming any kind of designer and that is the problem. I had no college career goal. I didn't have many hobbies or career interests. If my dad had still been in our home, I believe at least he would have cared enough to help me figure it all out. At the current time, though, I didn't want his help. I didn't want him to influence my future in any way.

"You know you should buy more clothes," Winter suggested. "Your old ones are kind of outdated." She began to show me different clothing items so that I could get an idea of what to buy.

That was when I noticed she had already piled a whole bunch of clothes over her arms. I didn't even want to think about how much all of that was going to add up to. *What can you expect from her, though? It is not as if she's worked a day in her life.* As people always say, "It's daddy's money."

"You know, not everybody has tons of money to spend on items they clearly don't need. Plus, I have to start saving up for college."

"Yes, you're right. I'm sorry. I keep forgetting that in a couple of months you will be abandoning me." Winter made a sad puppy face designed to manipulate me into feeling sorry for her — which I did, but not for the reason she'd intended.

"You are so pathetic. I am not even abandoning you. I am literally going to be living under the same roof as you, dummy." I tapped the tip of her nose and then began to make my way to the cash register so she would stop looking around for more clothes, and we could finally leave to get something to eat.

"First, don't call me pathetic," she said. "Second, can we just go home now? I'm starting to get hungry," Winter's face reddened as she nervously put all the clothes back on their racks.

"Aren't you going to get those clothes?" I was in shock and confused by what my eyes were telling me at that moment.

"Nah, I will be fine. Plus, your wise words made me reconsider my choices on how to spend my money," she said quickly and softly before she ran out of the store, leaving me behind.

"Alright, if you say so," I said, even though she wasn't there to hear it. I was so annoyed that we'd spent over an hour in that stupid store, and she didn't end up getting anything. *What a waste of my time!* I fumed. *I guess I asked for it, though.*

I still hadn't understood what was going on. Never before had I seen Winter walk out of a clothing store without a bag in her hands.

Actually, also I'd never before seen her that nervous. Something was going on, but clearly, she did not want to talk about it at the moment.

Immediately all thoughts of my sister fled at the sight of a mysterious young guy timidly walking alone around the clothing store. I must have never seen him before since I surely would have remembered such a peculiar face. It was too perfect, like the ones you see in the magazines or on billboards. He had straight brown hair and the lightest green eyes I had ever seen. Those eyes seemed to reflect everything he gazed upon. I had the overwhelming certainty that if I ever got the chance to know him, I would probably fall in love with him in an instant. Could this be love at first sight?

Call me young and naïve, but from what I saw right then, he was an easy person to read. He seemed to want to be seen, to be understood. But I wondered at his raw vulnerability. *What happened to him?* I wondered. *Who broke his heart?* There was no spark in his eyes, no excitement in his smile. He looked as if he was trying to get back the missing piece that he had lost only a few days before. I wanted to go

26

over there and give him a hug, but probably that would have weirded him out. Still, he sure looked as if he really needed a hug right there and then.

I wanted to reassure him and tell him that everything would be okay, that no matter what, he would get through it. He looked as if he had been battling so many wars all alone that he'd never even told anyone about. I wanted to be that anyone for him. I know it was crazy to think all these things about a stranger, about a guy I'd only just this once laid my eyes on, but in that moment, I could confidently say that I might have fallen in love — at last. *Could he be the one?*

"Summer, get yourself out here right now!" Winter yelled from the entrance of the store with an annoyed look on her face.

"Did you see that guy?" I asked, completely ignoring what she'd just said. After snapping out of my trance. I noticed the look of disappointment and disgust that had flashed across Winter's face after I asked about that mysterious guy. She clearly knew who I was talking

27

about. Why all of a sudden did she seem mad at me? "Wait, do you know that guy from somewhere?"

"Who are you even talking about?" she asked. "I didn't see any guys when I came in. I'm going to go get the car. You can just wait for me here if you want to. I don't care."

She didn't even give me the chance to respond as she made her way into the busy parking lot. I never thought I would see the day when Winter didn't acknowledge a pretty boy, especially one like this guy —slightly taller than I and with a very toned body. Someone like him, with his looks, must have been playing some kind of sport, and I judged him to be around our age. *Maybe she's telling the truth*, I thought. *Maybe she didn't see him Or maybe she is lying to me. Maybe he's the guy from summer camp she mentioned last week.* I had so many questions and no answers for them. I just wanted to know what was really going on. I wanted to know if it was safe for me to fall in love with a guy whom I didn't know anything about. *What if I fall in love with the wrong person?*

"You are Summer, right?" said a voice behind me. I turned around to see the mysterious guy standing right there and looking straight into my eyes. It kind of felt as if he was reaching right into my soul.

"Yes, how did you —"

"Your friend just yelled it from across the store," he said. He was not being a jerk. I could see that from the way he kept playing with his hands and clinching his jaw. *He is nervous to be here next to me,* I thought. *He is scared to talk to me, but why?*

"Actually, that was my sister. Do I know you from somewhere?" By asking this, I was hoping our conversation would eventually lead to a name so I could at least know some personal information about this guy. I didn't want him to figure out that I was attracted to him. That would have been just too embarrassing.

"Oh, that makes so much sense now," he answered with a look of disappointment as if Winter's being my sister was the worst thing he could have ever learned. "I was actually coming to bring you your phone. It fell out of your purse as soon as you began to walk out of the store. I was pretty sure you'd want it back as soon as you realized it was gone." He took my phone out of his pocket jacket, and right before handing it to me, quickly snatched a small piece of white paper with numbers written on it, cramming it back into his pocket.

We just stood there in silence for a couple of seconds. I had expected him to leave right after handing me my phone, but he didn't. I really wanted to ask him what was written on that slip of paper but was too scared. At least, if I had been brave enough to look into his eyes, maybe I could have figured out what he was thinking. All I really wanted to know was his name — and probably if he was going to our school that year. Otherwise that day could be the last time I would ever see him. *Is there even a chance for us to get to know each other?* I thought. Even though I wanted to know whether or not Winter knew this guy, deep down I feared the answer.

"Summer, get in here," Winter demanded as she pulled up next to us. Immediately after delivering this command, she rolled the window back up. Once again, although Winter was the youngest, she usually acted as if she was the one in charge.

"I'm sorry. I have to go," I said as I headed toward the car. At the same time, I realized that the guy had already started to walk away amid a huge crowd of loud teenagers.

"Did you know that guy?" I asked as soon as I closed the car door. The whole time I kept my eyes on her face, trying to read her facial expressions as she formed her answer.

"Why do you keep asking me the same thing over and over? I already told you that I didn't see any guys. What else do you want me to tell you?" She looked more annoyed than ever. I knew she was lying to me, but I still couldn't understand what was making her so angry. If this was the guy from camp she'd talked about the week before, she didn't have any right to be mad. She was the one who cheated on him. Technically, she didn't really love him. But then, she could still have had feelings for him and was just trying to convince herself — and everyone else — that she didn't.

31

Winter was clearly avoiding the topic, and I somewhat understood why. If I had broken an innocent guy's heart, I'd be avoiding that topic, too.

But I hated being so pushy with my questions, so I just decided to let the conversation go and focus on playing multiple songs on the radio's high volume until we arrived at home. *Now*, I thought, *I have to figure out a way to get at the truth without having to ask Winter for it.* After all, I didn't even know what his name could be. So, where could I start?

Chapter 2

The first day back to school was utterly chaotic. I barely got any sleep the night before because I kept thinking about that guy I didn't even know anything about. The uncertainty of Winter knowing him was making me so impatient with her. She woke up late that morning and didn't finish getting ready until 7:45 A.M.. Thank God we lived close to the school because if not, we would have been late on the first day of school, and nothing is more embarrassing than that. *Maybe, it's not embarrassing for Winter,* I mused. This wouldn't have surprised me because knowing Winter, she might have thought that being late would make her look cooler to her friends, but it was embarrassing to me. I was the one who had to run all across the school with the wrong

33

schedule in hopes of finding the right classroom before the bell rang. That morning, I made it just in time but resolved that if Winter was ever late again, she would have to walk to school, or she could ask one of her friends to give her a ride. They all had to drive by our house to get to the school anyway, so driving Winter really would not have been a problem for them.

I had forgotten how boring the first day back to school always was. Every single teacher had endless things to tell us such as: classroom rules, the material we are going to be covering, all the school material we will be needing, and grading with basically nothing else to do. At least that also meant I could focus my thoughts on something more interesting and important in the meantime. After all, I've been thinking about someone else for two days.

I just couldn't get *him* out of my mind. Every time I closed my eyes, I would see his face. I just wanted to be able to move on and forget about ever seeing him or ever talking to him. I felt so foolish for falling in love so easily with a stranger. I didn't even know who he was, and so far, all of my expectations about him could have been a lie. *Maybe I fell in love with the idea of him,* I wondered. *Maybe he is nothing like I think he is.* Maybe he hadn't been nervous because he was next to me. Maybe he was just being a good person by handing my phone back. On the other hand, maybe my worries were really true, and he was the mysterious guy Winter had talked to me about. She hadn't given me a name or any kind of description. *Dang, I don't even think she ever mentioned a single thing about him other than what she did to him.* I wished I could ask her more about it, but she had been acting weird since the day before.

She'd seemed so nervous on the ride home the night before. She didn't say a single word to me after we got home. On our way to school she was also mute. Maybe my worry had become reality. My sister might have ruined the only true relationship she has ever had. *What's worse is,* — the thought stuck in my throat— *we might be in love with the same guy.*

'ever noticed how social media can be useful and useless at the same time? I spent four hours looking for that guy, but all I could find were boys who I had already seen at school.

He is not from here, I concluded. If I was right about that, my job had become ten times harder because I didn't have a clue about where he was from! Knowing that made my challenge feel like finding a needle in a large field full of grass. In other words — impossible. My first love was impossible.

How did I get into this mess so quickly? I asked myself. *I don't want to fall in love. That is the last thing I want to do during my senior year of high school.* I hated the thought of dating men. I hated the thought of having to belong to someone else. Seeing the way all those guys had treated my sister made me reconsider so many things about my life. After my dad cheated on my mom, the last thing I wanted to do was fall in love. I didn't want to feel broken like mom did. I didn't want to feel betrayed like my sister did. *I don't want to endlessly cry over a boy who doesn't really love me,* I told myself. All I wanted was to be loved the way it happens in the movies. On the other hand, who was I kidding? In the past two years, I had come to learn that movies were all lies because modern-day love is so hurtful. No one has good intentions, and everyone is thinking about themselves. They are too selfish and self-absorbed to be capable of loving anyone else. *When did society change so drastically for the worse?* I agonized. *How can people settle for this insensitive dating culture?*

I knew I was not going to be able to find the kind of love I was looking for while I was still surrounded by so many immature adolescent boys who cared only about having sex with the hottest girls in school. I wanted a slow, sincere love. I wanted to be able to rely on not getting hurt. I didn't ever want to come home slamming the doors and running straight into my bedroom to cry my heart out because the boy I cherished had dumped me. In other words, I didn't want Winter's chaotic life. I didn't want to keep trying to find the one guy. Because he didn't exist in high school. And instead of finding him, I was just going to keep losing pieces of my heart to an endless string of wrong guys. I just want to be loved the right way. *Is that too much to ask? Is society going to call me too demanding?* For then, I decided I would stay single until someone made me feel safe enough to let all of my defenses down. I had just really thought for a slight second that yesterday's mysterious guy was going to be the one.

Crap, I have been camped inside my head all day. I didn't even realize that it was time to leave class to fulfill an obligation. I was happy for my sister to be involved with school and all, but I really wished I didn't have to be dragged along to all of her activities. We shared a car, so we always had to wait for each other unless one of us could manage to find another ride home.

After school that day was the first football game of the season, so right when the bell rang, people were starting to head out there to get a good spot to sit. I hated having to go. Technically, I was not being forced to go. I just had nothing else to do until my sister was finished cheerleading.

As I got up from my desk, I knocked everything onto the floor — my laptop, my phone, my books, and my notebooks. *What is going on with me?* I had never been so distracted at school — and certainly not that clumsy. When I examined my most expensive belongings — my phone and laptop — I was relieved to find no damage from the fall. At least this wouldn't be added to the list of my worries.

Right when I went to reach for the rest of my stuff, my hand touched someone else's. — a hand that I was not familiar with until I turned my head slightly to get a look at it. The moment I saw the scars imprinted in its skin, memories began to rush my brain. But how could that be possible? Some part of me didn't want to get too excited that I believed this guy was really right there in front of me. Was I so distracted to not even notice him sitting in the same room? *How stupid can I be?*

Before I could even say anything, he picked up the rest of my stuff from the floor and gave me his other hand to help me get back up. I never thought this would happen. *Technically, I am holding his hand right now,* I thought. Even though we were not romantically holding hands, my heart was overwhelmed with joy. *Am I being delusional right now? Or am I just daydreaming about him again?*

"You need to be more careful," he said as he looked me in the eyes and began to hand me back my stuff. "I am pretty sure your phone and laptop wouldn't be so cheap to repair if their screens had gotten broken," On that day, he was smiling. His eyes looked so different from the last time I saw him. They looked brighter, almost sparkly. *Could I be the reason his spark is back?*

"I know," I said. "I'm usually more careful about my phone. As you've probably already figured out, I can be clumsy when I am distracted," I began to make my way out of the classroom, all while hoping that he would follow along.

"Are you heading to the pep rally?" he asked before I got too far away. I could see that he was hoping I'd say yes, that he wanted me to go with him. I couldn't deny it; I wanted the same thing. *How is it that his name has not come across yet?* I didn't think I would have been so impolite, but once again, our generation could care less about manners.

"I was just going to sit in the car until it's over. I have to wait for my sister." I was trying so hard to hide how I felt. If I found him so easy to read, I never wanted to find out how easily *he* could read *me*. I didn't want to be that girl who jumps to conclusions and sees signs that aren't there just because she likes a guy. I wanted to see in his actions if he was really into me. At the same time, I wanted to spend more time with him. His face showed me that I had given him an answer he didn't want to hear. *Maybe this is all in my head,* I thought. *Maybe he's just lonely and wants to be friends with me.* I didn't think I could handle getting friendzoned so fast by the first guy I had ever liked. What if he was trying to be near me just to make Winter jealous? *Could that be a possibility?*

"Well, as you may already know," he said, "I am new to this school, and I really don't have any friends yet. You are basically the only person I know…"

Great, I was getting friendzoned already.

41

"Only if you do me a favor —" I interrupted him. I finally got my chance to ask him his name. I hoped he didn't think I was weird. I had never talked to a guy that I liked before. I had no clue what I was doing.

"What kind of favor?" He crossed his arms and looked at me up and down as he leaned half of his body against one of the lockers. He seemed curious to know what I was going to say next, but I worried that, he might be teasing me. *I guess he is not that different from any other guy.* It was strange that someone like him hadn't made any friends yet. I decided that I wouldn't be surprised if he was lying to me at that very moment. At least, I could see that he was starting to loosen up a little. However, it could be that he was the guy I'd thought he was. *Maybe this is a sign that I should stop talking to him,* I reasoned, *but what if I'm wrong? Is it too naive to want to be more than friends with someone who might break my heart?*

"Since you know my name, I think it would be fair for me to know yours." *I am finally getting his name,* I thought. *This is really going to happen. I mean, it only took me a day to find out on my own.* I would probably have gotten it faster from Winter if she hadn't been so secretive and dodged my questions about him, but now, nothing prevented me from learning his name. After all, Winter was not there to stop me.

"Oh, right. Sorry. I'm Liam." He stood up straight and reached his right hand forward for a hand shake as if it was our first time meeting each other. He spoke so confidently. I decided that my predictions about him had been wrong after all. He didn't seem to be shy at all. I guess I jumped to conclusions about him that day at the mall. I was wrong, and I can see that now.

"Nice to meet you, Liam." As his hand touched mine, I could feel the redness spreading over my face. His was so warm and large, compared to mine. All of a sudden, I wished I could see myself to make sure that at least I looked okay. As for him — he looked so cute as he was gazing at me. How did his hair manage to stay so perfect after eight hours in this school? Our school's air conditioning made my hair go from silky, bouncy curls to horrible, frizzy witch hair. For all I knew, at that very minute, I might have looked like a little lion. And not in a cute way. More like a scary version of a lion. Could it be that he didn't really care about my appearance that much?

Surely, he didn't have any reason to be smiling at me in that certain way. He could have chosen from any number of prettier girls in our class to talk to that day. Trust me, tons of girls were also much cooler than I in that school. I hoped he wouldn't end up going away the moment he realized that I am totally not fun at all. I bet he was a popular guy at his old school, and people like that don't hang out with people like me. *They think I am too boring.*

"Let's go before it gets too crowded," he suggested as he dropped my hand and began walking down the hall toward the door nearest the football stadium.

Why is HE the one leading the way? Wasn't he just complaining that he was new there and didn't have any friends? *Has he already decided to just leave me behind?*

"Wait up," I yelled from across the hall as I began to rush over next to him. I don't think he realized how fast he was walking.

His hair looked so shiny. The sun was beaming down on him, making his hair look golden brown and his eyes take on the shade of green that you could probably find only in the clearest sea water around small islands. I had always wanted to travel to places like that. *But, I thought, I might be satisfied with just looking into his beautiful eyes instead.* I didn't need anything else or want anyone else. *If I could just have him... Is it so bad that I desperately want to hold his hand at this very moment?*

As we speed walked side by side, our hands kept slightly rubbing against each other. He led me to an empty row of bleachers slightly away from the big crowd of loud and annoying teenagers. We might not have had the best view there, but we could at least talk to each other without any interruptions. I wondered if this was what he'd wanted from the start. *Stop it!* I told myself. *I can't let myself believe that Liam is really into me until he tells me he is.* It was scary to know how much I had come to like him in just two days. Already I couldn't imagine

45

being able to hide my true feelings and pretend mere friendship if it turned out that he wasn't into me at all.

Again, my thoughts returned to the worst situation of all, that this was the guy Winter talked to me about. In that case, ours would be more heartbreaking than a real breakup since Winter clearly still cared about him. *Surely, she would be jealous if I dated the person she loved.* I didn't want to be selfish about it, but I consoled myself with the thought that at least she hadn't said anything about him so far. And as my sister, she would usually tell me things that were as important as this. *So, in the meantime, I think there is nothing wrong for us to get to know each other, right?*

"You don't really like going to things like this, do you?" he asked after we had been sitting there in silence for the past couple of minutes. He was so right. I hated pep rallies as much as I hated going to football games. Part of this may be that my dislike of athletes was even greater than my hatred toward my dad. I lumped them all together as loud and annoying jerks. *I just don't get why they have to be so cocky just because they are popular.*

"Not really." I finally answered. I didn't know what else to say. *I am overthinking this too much...* The palms of my hands were getting too cold because of the windy weather, and being nervous wasn't helping my situation either. Trying to rub them together to create some heat was always so useless since I have tiny, bony hands. I wished I had thought to bring a jacket with me. I had one in my car, but I was too scared to leave him alone for even the couple of minutes it would take to go get it. Although he probably wouldn't mind. *It's not like he has said a word to me yet. I should be able to make it back before the rally is over, but I don't want him to think that I'm bailing out.*

"Are you cold? Here let me help." He grabbed both my hands and began to hold them tightly against his chest and then neck. *How can he stay this warm in such weather?* I thought. But don't get me wrong; I was not complaining. I was enjoying every minute of this closeness. My heart was beating so hard and fast, and I could feel the blood rushing through every part of my body. *I hope he can't hear it,* I thought nonsensically. *I hope he can't feel the fastness of my pulse in my fingers or the palms of my hands.* Okay, that thought felt more rational. I hoped he couldn't sense the shivers going through my body as my hands were against him.

I felt like I was running out of air. I couldn't breathe. *Oh, crap! I really can't breathe.* I didn't know what was happening — and then I began to. *I haven't had a panic attack in so long.* Actually, I had just stopped taking medication for my anxiety because I didn't need it anymore. *Sure, I barely got any sleep last night because I had a lot on my mind but that always happens the day before the new school year begins.* Then I remembered the way I had been stressing about Liam's identity for the entire day. On top of that, I was worrying about what Winter had been hiding from me those past days.

All right, so the attacks have come back. But please not now, of all times — not while I'm sitting next to him. Not while he is trying to do something nice for me. He is going to think that I am going nuts or that I am fangirling over him. I can't do this right now. Still, I felt so lightheaded and as if I had a knot in my throat. I wanted to let him know what was happening so that I wouldn't end up scaring him off. The problem was that I couldn't speak. My breathing was so labored. *Oh, great! Now I'm crying. What the hell is wrong with me?*

"Summer, just breathe, okay? Just follow me. Inhale," he said, breathing in slowly as he counted to three, "Exhale." He let a big breath out of his mouth for about five more seconds and then did the same thing over and over again until I was able to breathe normally on my own. He then wiped away the tears from my face and gave me the sweetest hug I have ever received from anyone who was not a family member.

How did he know what was happening to me? *Maybe he knows someone who gets them too. Maybe he gets them too.* No one had ever been successful at calming me down as quickly as he did. My parents and even Winter had tried many times when I was younger but always seemed to make it worse. No one seemed to know what to do.

"How are you feeling?" Liam asked.

I was amazed at how concerned he was about my wellbeing. His face clearly showed fear and worry in. *He has a big, kind heart. I can see that.* If my thoughts were correct about him and Winter, I was determined not to let Winter get close to him ever again. *She broke this boy's heart. She broke this sweet and caring guy's heart. Why? Why would she do that?* If this was true, I was going to do everything in my power to protect him from her at all costs — even if it meant that my little sister would hate me for the rest of our lives.

"I'm okay," I whispered. But I was definitely not okay. I felt so nauseous and lightheaded. I also had so much worry in my heart. It hurt to carry all of that and not be able to talk to anyone about it. I wished I was brave enough to tell him the truth, but I was not.

"We can leave if you want to" Liam said. "I'll take you home." He hoisted my backpack from the floor and put it over his left shoulder. He then offered both of his hands to help me get up. But as soon as I took my first step, I lost all of my balance and was about to head for the worst fall of my life down the stairs — before Liam quickly caught me. At that moment, our faces were so close to each other. For the first time, I looked straight into his eyes and for a quick second allowed my gaze to linger on his lips. I wondered how they tasted, how they would feel on my lips. I wanted to kiss him, but if I'd had time to really think about it, I never would have wanted my first kiss to be that way. After all, I had known him for less than a week. It was way too early for that to happen.

Suddenly, a couple of teenagers appeared, and Liam began to pull away from me slowly and discretely. He was being careful with every move, every gesture, and every word. *How can I not fall for him?*

As soon as we got to his car, he opened the door for me and placed my backpack in the backseat. His black car was just the way I would have envisioned it. The seats were all shiny and clean. The inside of the car smelled like new. The floorboard had zero trash, and on the backseat a neat stack of notebooks was organized. *He definitely cares about what people think of him. He also seems to be the type of guy Winter usually dates. I wonder what else I've guessed wrong about him. I'd love to be wrong in my suspicions about Winter and him, but I won't let myself just assume that — no matter how much I hope it to be so.*

"Do you want to play music?" Liam asked before turning the engine on. He began to look through his phone — probably to get some ideas just in case I didn't have anything in mind, but I actually did — not a particular song, but definitely a vibe.

"Can you please play something with summer vibes?" I said, in hopes he would be interested.

"Coming right up, *Summer* vibes," Liam said with an odd emphasis on "summer."

I guess he was trying to be funny about it. I could relate. My name is pretty much what I love the most about every year. If I ever had the chance to change my name, I wouldn't. I want to make people feel the same way summer makes me feel. In my opinion, summer can be therapeutic, and nowadays people badly need and want its sense of happiness and freedom. People need excitement and adventures. People also need the way summer draws us to the ocean and its creatures, to the sun and salty air. The whole summer vibes just describe who I am as a person, and I want people to know that. When they look at me, I want them to think of summer. I want to bring them joy.

We stayed pretty quiet for the rest of the ride home. Since I could play navigator, it took only about ten minutes to get there — but still enough time to listen to three of my favorite songs. Seeing the way he so naturally chose my favorite music and artists made me feel as if we had been friends for ages. Considering I'd met him only the day before and had learned his name only hours ago made it is strange that I could feel so close to him. It seemed as if he knew me more than I knew myself and understood me in ways no one had ever been able to.

As he parked in front of my house, I was overwhelmed with the desire to stay much longer in that car. But I was also torn. I had nothing to do at home, but also, I was scared to be seen with him because of the whole Winter complication. Since probably the pep rally was well over, she would be home any minute. All that remained to say between us was "see you tomorrow," but some part of me wanted to hear him pose the question: "Do you want to hang out sometime?"

"I'll see you tomorrow, right?" he said. I took this as my hint to start getting out of his car.

"Yes," I said, reaching over the seat to get my backpack. Before I could open the door, I realized that my sister had just arrived home. *How the hell did she get here so fast? She is the slowest driver I have ever met.*

"See you tomorrow." With that, I shot out of his car and toward the house so that I could avoid seeing Winter's face. *She is either going to be really happy and curious about this new guy who just drove me home, or she is going to go nuts about seeing me with her "possible" ex-boyfriend from summer camp. If so, does she think she can keep avoiding the truth forever?*

Chapter 3

For an hour and a half, I could hear Winter throwing and breaking stuff in her room. Our rooms were separated by only a thin wooden wall. When we were little, I used to enjoy that. But having to listen to this madness nonstop completely changed my mind. *If she doesn't stop soon, she's going to regret breaking so much stuff, that she likes. But then again, she'll probably just go on a shopping spree tomorrow after school to replace everything she broke. I wouldn't be surprised if she is already planning to do that.* I expected that after all the noise was over, she would start screaming and sobbing like an infant. She really needed help, and I wanted to help her.

What stood in my way was fear that I was the cause of her anger. I didn't want to end up getting yelled at — or worse getting hit — for something I had no idea I was doing. *Hopefully, she will eventually calm down soon. At least, I will be the first one to know when she does.* Our mom was going to be home from work in less than an hour. I didn't think she would want mom to see her in such a state. She never cried in front of mom. Maybe it was because she didn't want to seem pathetic in our mother's eyes. She certainly never sought her help or comfort either.

Winter always turned to me for that. Maybe that was why she was so hurt. She had been struggling to talk to me about things, and at that point, she probably thought that I had betrayed her. But then I didn't even know if that was true. *I'm going to give her another thirty minutes to calm down before I go in there and look at all the damage. I hope she doesn't have anything else to throw, especially at me.*

Around ten minutes later, the noise stopped. I was not trying to avoid anything or pretend like nothing had happened. I was just terrified to see her face right at that moment. Why I was so scared, I wasn't sure. Winter might have been impulsive, but she had never been aggressive or emotionally unstable. Knowing that, I should have been in there next to her. Instead, I found myself sitting on the floor next to my full-size bed, holding my phone.

How did I not think of looking up Liam on social media when I got back home from school? Right, I was running away from having to face Winter. Once online, I could finally see if he was who I thought he was. I remember suspecting that Winter knew Liam, and her recent behavior just confirmed my suspicions. A part of me wished it was not true, though. All of this could have been prevented if Winter had just told me who her ex-boyfriend was from the start.

I didn't realize that the world had so many Liams. Finding this guy's information or contacts seemed impossible. *Wait a minute, what if he did go to summer camp with Winter? The camp always took pictures of the campers and posted them on their account.* As I began to type the account username, my fingers started shaking. My eyes began to droop as I felt how tired I was — and all of the sudden lightheaded and nauseous as

57

well. My stomach was twisting and rolling from one side to the other. *I'm just really nervous. It can't be another anxiety attack!* I kept telling myself to calm down, that whatever the truth was, it wouldn't be as bad as I had made it be. For all I knew, my suspicions could have been wrong.

For five minutes, I had been scrolling through their account, all the time stressed that Winter would walk in at any moment. If didn't she saw what I was doing, it would have made it hard to claim that I hadn't been aware of the situation in any way.

Pictures of Winter and her friends are everywhere but none of them with any guy. In my last attempt, I decided to see if the account was tagged on anyone's post. I couldn't believe what I saw. Liam had volunteered at that same summer camp. My eyes were starting to tear up as my heart shattering piece by piece. I could no longer deny that they knew each other. *Winter knows Liam. Liam knows Winter, and he probably already knew who I was from the beginning.* Winter didn't want to talk about it because she was embarrassed. But seeing her older sister talking to her ex-boyfriend, made her want to kill the whole world around her. At this point, I had to hear the truth from both of them — or at least from Winter. *She is my sister. She owes it to me.*

"So, I see you've met him," Winter stood right in my doorway, looking down at me. My door had been closed. How did I not hear her come in? "Come on, you don't have to lie to me about it," she went on, "especially not about him." She walked forward and sat next to me on the floor.

I was still too scared to speak. Besides, I had never been put in that kind of situation before and didn't know what to say. *But she's my little sister, after all,* I repeated to myself. Up to that time, we'd trusted each other more than anyone or anything. I realized then that things were meant to change, and no one could stop that from happening.

Even as Winter had begun to approach me, she was looking to see what I was doing on my phone, but I was too fast for her. I had already turned it off as soon as I saw her standing by the door. On the outside, she appeared quiet. Her mind, on the other hand, not that much. I could somehow sense that.

"Oh, were you doing your research?" Winter asked, grabbing my phone. When she unlocked it, the screen where I had left off appeared: Liam's account. "When I saw you two at the pep rally, I thought I was going crazy for a minute." Scrolling through Liam's photos, she stopped at one particular image and began to analyze every single little detail of his face.

"I wanted to tell you who he was," Winter began. "When we were at the mall and you asked me if I knew him, I was still shocked from running into him. After he saw me and this other guy kissing, he drove out of the camp before we could say anything to each other —" *I don't know what she wants me to say, but I guess it doesn't matter because she isn't giving me time to say anything.* "I understood why he did it though. I knew what he felt the moment he caught us. I knew how heartbroken and angry he was . . ."

She kept pausing after every sentence, but then would add something else right when I was going to respond. I could see that she was planning something, but I didn't know what she had on her mind.

She seemed to be having trouble with what to say next as if she was scared of saying the wrong thing. And yet, she just kept plodding on.

"You see Summer, when you are in love, that is your worst nightmare. Boys have dumped me, and now I have done that to him. I felt so bad for a couple of days — until I saw him entering the clothing store. That's when I realized how much I still love him. I still love Liam in my own, difficult way. I just know that he is never going to forgive me for — that other thing. I messed up. I know I suck. I just didn't think he was really into me like I was into him.

I was scared he was going to break up with me as soon as summer camp was over. What's worse is… he probably convinced his parents to let him go to our school just to be with me, and now… he goes to the same school, and we are not even together anymore. Summer, I don't know what to do. I really love him." She sat closer to me on the floor. After beginning to cry, she threw her arms around me. She was holding onto me tightly, her body shaking from distress. All the tears that she had been trying to hide were running freely from her eyes. Her round face, almond eyes, and small nose had become bright red.

I believed her. Every single word she said was true. Winter never lied to me. My worst fear had become a reality. As I realize this, my mind was filled with accusations. *I should have been there for her. I should have volunteered whenever she asked me to. I should have forced her to tell me what was going on. I should have spent more time with her. I should have talked to her more.* I wish she had come to me for advice and just told me what was going on in her life. If she had just told me the truth from the start, all of this mess would have not happened in the first place.

~

Two years before, Winter had fallen in love for the first time. She was in middle school, and I was in high school. Even though we didn't see each other a lot, still, after school, we would tell each other all kinds of stories about our day. We did our homework together, watched movies together, ate together, and talked nonstop about boys together. Our bond was stronger than ever. Winter's boy problems

62

began one Friday evening. All the love and chaos had unfolded in that specific moment when she told me that she was asked to go on a date.

"Summer!" Winter had screamed as she ran toward me from across the school's parking lot.

"Be careful, Winter," I yelled in return. She was running in between cars. I didn't want a jerk to come out of nowhere and run over her.

"Omg. Omg. Omg. I need to tell you something." Winter held onto my arm to be able to catch her breath. She was all sweaty, and her ponytail had completely fallen out. Her blonde straight hair had never been as messy as it was at that moment. "Sam asked me out," she burst out.

"Sam? The Sam you've been drooling over for months?" I was actually surprised. *Do guys in middle school have the guts to ask a pretty girl out nowadays? He's a lucky one.*

"Let's go. You have to help me get ready," She ordered, running to the other side of the car and plopping into the passenger seat.

The whole drive home, Winter told me all about the way Sam had asked her out. In the last period, he'd passed her a note that said: *'Hey, Winter. There is a cool movie coming out tonight in the theater. Do you want to go and watch it with me?'*

How did she get so lucky? Winter was in the eighth grade and was already going on her first date while I had never been asked out by a boy in my life. I felt pathetic. I was the oldest, and it felt as if my little sister was going to be ahead of me with boys.

So for me, watching her leave that night was melancholic. On the one hand, I felt jealous and embarrassed. On the other hand, I was hopeful that one day it was going to be me and that I was going to look as beautiful as she looked.

In spite of those contradictory feelings flooding my mind, I helped her make waves in her golden hair and applied very light makeup on her face. She was wearing a soft pink blouse and light blue jeans. I wasn't worried at all about her wellbeing. This Sam guy looked like a nice person. Plus, Winter had known him since elementary school. They were not best friends, but at least they had known each other pretty well.

When she came back from her date, she was the happiest I had ever seen her. She played love songs from her phone and danced to them in her room. The moment I walked in, she dragged me into the crazy dancing. We continued to dance all night long until we had to stop out of exhaustion. Before we went to sleep, she told me she thought that Sam was *the one*. She was falling in love with him. She told me how great he had treated her the whole night. He'd paid for the tickets and the food. He'd kissed her on the cheek while they were waiting for his brother to arrive to give them a ride back to our house. And right then and there, he'd asked her out again. Without hesitation, my little sister said yes, of course.

Winter and Sam dated for a year before they broke up. It was the sweetest relationship I had ever seen in real life. They were so cute together. When she told me what had happened, I didn't want to believe her. It was too devastating to believe that someone like Sam would do something like that. They loved each other — or at least, that is what everyone thought.

I remember that horrible night so well that my blood starts to boil every single time I think of it. Winter came back from a friend's party at 9 p.m.. That is the only time she had ever come home from a party before midnight. I looked outside my window to see her getting out of a black Nissan, a car I didn't recognize. She had ridden to the party with Sam and his older brother. Sam always promised to get her home safe so I couldn't figure out the strange car.

The moment she came into the house, I knew something bad had happened. Winter was standing by the front door, looking pale, as if she was about to throw up. She looked angry as well. Her hair was all frizzy and tangled. Her face had scratches and so did her arms. Did she get into a fight? If so, with whom?

"Winter, what happened?" I asked in hopes of getting information out of her. The eyes I peered at had lost their shine. Her whole face looked so unalive. *Whoever hurt her deserves to go to hell,* I fumed.

"He cheated on me." She let out a big cry and dropped to her knees. She held onto my legs and kept saying things I could barely hear or understand.

"Slow down," I soothed. "Please, calm down. Just tell me what happened." I kneeled in front of her and looked into her teary blue eyes as I held her hands close to my chest.

"I had to use the bathroom," she began but then seemed to choke at the words. Clearly, she still was too upset to relate events in her usual nonstop fashion. Eventually I got from her — after starts and stops — that her trip to the bathroom had taken so long that she was afraid that Sam was going to think she had left the party. When she returned to the living room, she couldn't find him anywhere. His brother and friends were still there talking to some girls, but Sam wasn't anywhere she could think to look, including the backyard and inside every room in the house.

"I thought maybe he had gotten bored so went to see if he was waiting for me in the car. That's when I saw him kissing another girl," Winter paused to take a deep breath. "Summer, he was making out with another girl. I completely lost it."

She had banged on the windows until he came out of the car. Then she proceeded to yell at him and the girl. When Sam told Winter how sorry he was, she began to hit him and hit the girl, too. People from the party had to break them apart.

"I wanted to hurt them!" Winter cried "I wanted them to die. Sam had never treated me that way. He never paid attention to anyone but me. I just don't understand what I did wrong. I loved him so much. I gave him everything, Summer. Why would he do this to me? Why? Why!" Winter kept yelling and started to pull her hair out from anger.

Her hands were shaking because she was so mad at herself and at Sam. I felt her pain. I felt angry for her. I felt sad for her. If I could have taken the pain away, I would have. But instead, I just held her close to me until she didn't have any more tears to cry. It was the longest night of our lives. That was her first true love, her first heartbreak, her first betrayal.

~

I never thought she could ever hurt anyone the way she was hurt that night. *Did she already forget the longest night of her life and how devastating it was? Did she forget all the tears she cried and all the anger she felt? Did she forget how much it hurt to be betrayed by the person she loved the most? Why would she want someone to feel the same way? It doesn't make any sense.* "Winter. If you still love him, why haven't you talked to him and told him how you really feel?" Even though I didn't want Winter and Liam to get back together, I also didn't want to come between them. They had history. Liam and I didn't.

"I've tried so many times, Summer. Ever since we ran into him, I have been calling him and texting him nonstop. He doesn't reply to texts or pick up the phone. He clearly doesn't want to talk to me so what else am I supposed to do?" She turned back to looking at Liam's pictures on my phone. She seemed to be mulling over an idea that she was scared to bring up.

"How do you two know each other?"

And there it was.

"We have class together," I answered, starting to think that Winter was not the kid I used to know. Suddenly she seemed all grown up. She wanted things and didn't need me to get them for her anymore. She could do it on her own now. *No way is she going to ask me to help her out with Liam. Anyway, I don't think I could do that for her, not while I am still in love with him.*

"Can you please tell him to look at the text messages I've sent him?"

She was up to something. Her eyes were opened wide, and she looked excited. *She thinks this is going to work out. She thinks Liam is going to forgive her after he reads those messages. What am I going to do if he does? Am I just going to sit there and see what happens next?*

"Sure. I'll try."

Of course I didn't want to, but what kind of sister would I have been if I turned her down? Last week, all I wanted was to reconnect with my sister. I wanted to be a good sister to Winter and was willing to learn the things she liked to do. *Now, I just feel jealous of her.* After all, Winter loved the guy I loved, but she didn't deserve him. *She had her chance and lost it, said the little devil on my shoulder. It is not fair for her to get a second chance. It's not fair because I want to be with him.*

"Thank you so much!" She gave me a quick hug and began to walk out of my room. Before she closed the door behind her, she stopped to look back at me. All at once, I could see in her eyes. *She knows I like Liam. She knows that the whole situation is bothering me.*

"Summer," Winter said, leaning against the doorjamb.

71

"Yes?" I looked up at her.

"It's girls' code to not date each other's boyfriends," she said. "Just so you know." Then she abruptly closed the door, leaving me no chance to respond.

I had never been so confused about my own little sister. *Why would Winter say something like that and then leave? Why would she ignore my feelings for Liam and care only about her own?* I knew the girls' code. Everyone did. I understood that it is all about loyalty, but ours was a whole different situation.

Their relationship had been a fling. She'd never expected it to last long term, even if he wanted it to. *She cheated on him, and now she says that she is truly in love with him? Who does that? Who cheats on someone they love? Who wants to hurt the person they are supposed to take care of?*

I'd thought Winter was a good person. Even then I knew she had good in her. But I also felt that her wanting to have Liam back after everything she made him go through was just selfish, and she knew it. She didn't care about my feelings, and I suspected that she didn't care about Liam's either. *Why can't she just move on to someone else like she always does? Why does she keep insisting on wanting to have Liam back?*

At that point, I wondered if I was just being paranoid about everything. I knew that one day Winter was going to find a good guy and then be the one who screwed things up. Of course, everything would have been so much simpler if I hadn't liked the same guy she liked. *I know what I have to do. I just wish things had been different from the start.*

Chapter 4

A month and a half had passed since I last spoke to Liam. Sometimes I felt bad for him. Many times during class he'd tried to begin conversations with me, but I just kept shutting him down. I hated having to do that, but part of me knew that it was the right thing to do — even though Winter and Liam hadn't gotten back together.

Actually, I didn't think he had spoken to her at all. The last time I heard Winter talk about him was that day after school when she made it clear to me how she still felt about Liam. She also made it very clear that I was not to come between them. *I hope one day she realizes how much this hurt me. She is aware of her actions just as much as she is aware of my feelings for Liam.* The fact remained and always will that I wasn't the one who met him first, who fell in love with him first, or who got the chance to be with him. *I was never part of the equation — until now.*

So far, my plan had been working, though. Little by little, as the days went by, my interest for Liam kept diminishing. I had been trying so hard to stay away from him at school as much as I could. I had even been making sure that my mind was free from any tempting thoughts about him. As a result, about a month ago I stopped daydreaming about what life could have been if we were together. *It's good that these things aren't happening with Liam because they are forbidden. I'm glad I placed this barrier between us. What was I even thinking before?*

In a couple of months, I would graduate; and in the meantime, I was working full-time. I didn't have time to be committed to a romantic relationship. Besides, dating would lead to a lot of expenses that I could not afford.

I needed to save my money for college. It was the only way I could have a better life than my mother's. It was the only way I could make sure to give my family a good life in the future. I was determined that they would never lose everything because Daddy took it away. I would be able to give my children a good life — with or without a husband. Hopefully, then they would be proud of me instead of feeling sorry for me. They could live life to the fullest while still having responsibilities. For me, everything in life has to have a balance between a little bit of goodness, like having fun, and a little bit of badness, like boring responsibilities, to be able to work out.

My sister and I are a great example of having an unbalanced life since we both lean too far on the opposite ends of the scale. My sister lives life to the fullest without any sense of responsibility or stress while I am so excessively responsible and anxious that it ends up sucking the life out of me. Neither of us has found a balance within our chaotic lives. Though so different, we both are failing in the other areas of life that we don't tend to look over or even spend time on.

At an early age, I was cut out and left to fend for myself. On the other hand, at the age of 15 my sister was still being guided step by step. I hadn't had any fun since our parents' divorce while my sister was

76

able to indulge in all the fun a teenager could have. It was as if she was having the best time of her life — for the both of us. I was not mad at her, though. I couldn't be since all of this was out of her control. The second I told mom about his affair, Dad switched his favor to Winter and away from me — the one he hated for ruining his marriage and his little fun adventure. He made sure to let me know how much he preferred Winter by spoiling her every week with all the money he could spare.

But of course, Winter didn't even know what happened. Mom and Dad agreed to tell her that they were splitting up was because they didn't love each other anymore. Winter believed it all — not because it came out of my mother's mouth but because instead, Dad stepped up to tell her all the pretty lies. From that time on, Dad did a better job of keeping his personal life a secret so that Winter wouldn't find out the truth.

Some part of me couldn't believe that Winter hadn't figured it out by then. *Maybe she does know but doesn't want to bring it up until one of them does. Or maybe Dad told her one day, and she forgave him.* It had been two years since our parents' divorce, and my anger hadn't lessened one bit. How could I forgive him when I saw him kissing a woman who was not my mom? He knew what he was doing. He knew he was hurting mom. He knew he was hurting both Winter and me, and he still chose to do it. *He doesn't deserve my forgiveness,* I thought. *He doesn't deserve Winter's either.*

Liam didn't seem to care that much that I'd been ignoring him. At first, I could see it was bothering him, but as the weeks went by, I guess he realized what was happening. After all, from the beginning, he knew I was Winter's sister. In the meantime, I had come to a place where I could be fine if he decided to get back with Winter. True, I still considered it the stupidest thing a person could do. However, if he still loved her, he should have been willing to give Winter another chance. She seemed to be really sorry about the whole situation. She also admitted to having feelings for Liam after all.

Maybe they should get back together. Maybe I should finally help Winter as she had asked me to, but who am I kidding? I couldn't bring myself to do that. I was a little bit selfish about him, too. I didn't think I could stand seeing him at our house kissing Winter. Nor could I have shared a car with them as they flirted throughout the entire ride. Every time I thought about them, my chest would hurt, and I would literally feel as if the life had drained out of me.

I was determined that they would never know about all this. In fact, I spent great effort to make sure that Liam would never find out about my feelings for him. If he ever did, I was afraid he might have changed his mind about my sister; and I wasn't going to take him away from her. *If it means that my sister is finally going to find happiness with the guy she loves, I am willing to risk it all for her.* Besides, for all I knew, my prince charming was waiting for me in my next chapter of life.

Ever since all my focus shifted from getting to know Liam to trying to avoid him at all costs, my life had been so boring. Days at school just crept by as I fell into the same old routine of listening, taking notes, and doing class work. Of course, if I'd had anyone talk to, the days would have gone by so much faster. But for two years I hadn't talked to any of my old friends. After my parents' divorce, I shut down and stopped talking to people and attending my club meetings. I even left the volleyball team. None of my friends knew what was going on and didn't recognize the person I had become. As much as they tried to help me, I kept pushing them away. All I wanted was to be alone.

Unfortunately, after all of this with Liam and Winter, being alone was the last thing I wanted. I needed a friend to talk about what was going on — someone to give me sincere advice. Maybe if I had been able to hear the perspective of someone removed from the situation, things would have made so much more sense to me. More than anything, I needed to be reassured that I was doing the right thing, that I wasn't making mistakes I might regret later on. *But who can I talk to when I have no one to rely on besides Winter?*

"Summer, is it okay with you if we all meet after school at the coffee shop down the street?" Liam asked. I looked up to see him with a girl and another guy —grouped around my desk and all looking down at me, waiting for my answer.

"Sure."

Because I didn't want Liam to know that I hadn't been listening to the teacher during class, I'd just agreed to something I had no clue about.

"Great," Liam said as he gathered up his stuff to leave. "Don't be late, guys."

Class is over already? I thought we just started. At least, that is how it felt to me. *No way did I lose track of time. What am I supposed to do?* I didn't get anything that was discussed. I didn't even know why we had to meet after school. *Are we doing a group project? If we are, how did Liam and I end up in a group with people who couldn't care less about school?*

As soon as I got up from the desk, I began to text Winter about not being able to go home immediately and that she should go on without me. Actually, since she had cheerleading practice, it wouldn't be much of an issue anyway. But I could still see a problem looming ahead. *I'm going to have to ask mom to pick me up instead so Winter won't see me with Liam. She'd probably think we were on a date!*

After my last class, I started to walk down the street to the coffee shop Liam had mentioned. Ten minutes after sitting down, I was still the only one there. I hadn't eaten anything all day, and the smell of freshly baked cookies was making me hungry. The shop was full of people, mostly young adults sipping their hot coffees or Frappuccinos. *I really want a Frappuccino right now.* I kept forgetting to bring my water bottle with me to school, so hadn't had anything to drink, either.

"Sorry I'm late." Liam placed his backpack on the chair next to him and sat down. He began to look around for the others. Unfortunately, it was just the two of us. "Are the other two not here yet?"

"Did you really think they were going to come?" I asked, rolling back my eyes. "They probably went on home." Out of my backpack, I began to take my laptop and a piece of paper and pen.

"So, have you thought about which country you want to write about?" he said, taking a notebook out of his backpack and searching for what turned out to be that day's class notes.

"Can we choose whichever we want?" I said, still trying to hide how distracted I'd been during class. *Just how long can I keep this up?* I wondered.

"You really weren't listening, were you?" Liam, annoyed, closed his notebook and looked at me accusingly.

He's known all along. How stupid can I be?

"I'm sorry." I began to pack up to leave. *He is clearly mad at me for all the times I've deliberately ignored him. But none of this happening right now is my fault. I'm not the one who put us in a group together. If he wants to have this kind of attitude, he can just do the whole project by himself.*

"Where are you going?" He grabbed my arm and signaled me to sit back down. "I'm sorry, but you've been dodging me for the past month, and I'd like to know why."

83

Uncomfortable is a mild description of what I felt in that moment. In my mind, this was the last place and the wrong moment to talk about that subject. *Why does he have to be so incredibly straightforward? Can't he at least wait until we're finished with this project?*

"I haven't been." I said, determined to keep lying about it. *He can't know the truth of my forbidden love for him. He can't know that I am related to his ex. If he doesn't bring Winter into the conversation, I certainly don't have to.*

"That's bullshit." His fists began to tighten as his stare became even more intimidating.

One month ago, I didn't think Liam and I would ever talk again even though that is all I wanted to do. Finally finding myself with the chance to talk to him, and I was scared of just being with him! All I wanted to do was leave.

"I am sorry," he said, hiding his face in his hands. His body seemed so incredibly tense and rigid. His eyes betrayed that he hadn't slept well for days. I wanted to know what had been going on in his life.

I wanted to know if he had been thinking about Winter — or about me — at all.

"It's fine," I replied. "Let's just start working on this because those two are never going to show up." I began to pull up my laptop to type in a country and realized that I still didn't know which country we were supposed to research for the project. "By the way, which country are we doing?"

"Italy."

Out of all of the countries in the world, Italy was my favorite. Its people create the most exquisite pastries and dishes in the world. I had always wanted to visit Italy. But for the past two years, my plans had been shifting farther and farther away. Visiting that country was becoming more of a dream than a goal — mostly because I couldn't afford to go there — at least for a while. Any money I could've scraped up had to go toward college, and then after college, I would either have no money left or, in the worst-case scenario, end up with a lot of debt.

To sum it up, my priorities had shifted from discovering other parts of the world to saving every penny I earned so that in the future I could be earning more. Deep down, I knew that doing this all by myself was going to be very difficult in some ways, but alone it would have to be. I didn't expect to find someone willing to be with me and also capable of supporting my dreams financially and emotionally.

"I have never really looked into Italy's history or culture, so everything is kind of new to me," I began after a couple of minutes of quiet as we dived into our laptops.

"I've been there a couple of times during my childhood," Liam said, taking a mouthful of the sandwich. "It's pretty cool. You should definitely go one day if you can."

"I guess I should... maybe you can be my tour guide," I said in a quiet tone. All of a sudden, my face felt red, and I became small and shy as I looked at him over my laptop's screen.

"Only if you want me to. And if you do, then all this research will prepare us for our future trip."

As we diligently searched, we were learning about their political system and their family values, which are so different from the ones we have in the United States. We were also learning about their religion and their cuisine's history. *Everything has been going so well! This is too good to be true since I so much enjoy being with him.* I liked seeing the serious look on his face when he was reading articles. I loved seeing the spark in his eyes when he found something interesting and then showed it to me. *I don't mind that he's so quiet and focused. We're getting the job done, and that's all that matters. Maybe if we finish soon enough, we can talk or do something later.* After all that time sitting around in a coffee shop — surrounded by a variety of yummy smells — and yet not getting anything from the menu, I was extremely hungry.

"Alright, I guess we're done." Liam proclaimed and began to put all of his belongings back in his bag. After he finished, he sat straight up with his hands behind his head and started looking at me, as if for a signal.

But I wasn't ready to leave just yet. We'd spent only an hour working on the project. I wanted to spend more time just talking to him. *I doubt Winter is going to come by the coffee shop at this time, and if she does, she always goes through the drive-thru anyway. Still, why do I feel so guilty about all of this?* True, I had basically promised not to be involved with Liam. Still, she never mentioned that we couldn't be friends. Maybe at some point I would get the chance to ask him about what really happened between them.

"Are you hungry?" Liam asked. pulling his wallet out of a pocket.

"Kind of." For some reason, I didn't want him to know how hungry I was. *He doesn't know that I haven't eaten anything today, so if I eat too much, he's going to get the wrong impression.* Just then I remembered that I didn't have anything to eat at home. It had been two days since my mom had given me two hundred dollars to buy what we needed for that week, but I still hadn't gotten the chance to run by the grocery store. I'd have to either go grocery shopping or buy dinner out. *If I want to spend more time with him, I'm going to have to eat here. For now, that is basically my only option,* I thought, just then remembering that I didn't have a car.

"What do you want? I'll get it for you." He looked over and began reading the menu on the wall.

"It's okay. You can go ahead and order something while I look at the menu online," I said unlocking my phone. I already had an idea of what I wanted but also knew that what I wanted was not going to be very fulfilling — considering how ravenous I was feeling.

"If you say so," Liam said, heading toward the counter.

After a few minutes, I finally gave up. *Everything is so expensive here. And it's not even real food — just drinks and snacks loaded with sugar.* They had sandwiches and chicken wraps, but I was not willing to pay ten dollars for just one — especially since I didn't know how big they were. I was afraid that if they turned out to be like the ones at the grocery store, I probably wouldn't be able to stop myself from throwing a fit.

"Here you go." Liam sat down with what appeared to be two sandwiches, two chicken-and-bacon wraps, two iced-vanilla coffees, and two waters.

"This is a lot of food. There is no way you're going to eat all of that on your own." I had never before seen a person consume that much in one sitting.

"You are silly sometimes, but it's adorable. I wanted to buy you food but didn't know what you like so I got a bit of everything." Smiling at me, he placed a straw in each of our iced coffees.

"Thank you so much. I'll just take whatever." I said, trying hard not to blush. *He just said I am adorable! Wait — he said that my silliness is adorable. . . Never mind.*

"Here you go," he said, handing me one of the sandwiches and a water bottle. "So, what are your plans after graduation?"

"I am going to go to a community college and then transfer to a university. I still don't know what I want to do. I'm just going to go with the flow until something comes up." Just then it hit me that trying to eat and talk at the same time is not a very attractive look on anyone. *Maybe this will discourage him from having feelings for me.* "What about you?"

"I'm going to go to med school."

At that answer, I almost choked. *How smart and determined he must be to have chosen that career path!* I was already complaining about having to go to school for four more years after high school, and he was willing to do more than six years! *Oh, hell no. I guess at least he will be making a lot of money. Not just that — 'he'll be saving people's lives.*

"Why that reaction?" He was laughing softly as he reached for his first sip of coffee. *His jawline is so sharp right now. It could probably slice me in half. I have forgotten how perfect his smile is. It feels so warm and comfortable here all of a sudden.* I hoped that day would never end — or at least that we could have more days like it. *What am I thinking? This is already risky enough. Winter could find out about this in so many different ways.*

"I just never would have expected that answer from you. Why med school?" I hoped he didn't have a sad reason behind it. Almost every doctor I knew personally had chosen that profession because someone dear to them had passed away. Some people see it as a way to be useful while at the same time to fill the void created by grief. Though these are wonderful reasons, I didn't think I could handle a sad story right then.

"My sister passed away a couple of years ago after a car accident," he began. "I wasn't in the car with them. My mom was able to make a full recovery, but my sister was too injured to survive. I just wish I could have done something for her other than sit there and watch her slowly die. She was really young and never got to experience the things I have. It wasn't fair. I sometimes wish it had been me in that car instead. Life hasn't been easy at home since she passed away." As Liam slowly ate the rest of the food, his eyes began to tear up a little. I didn't think I had ever seen someone's eyes become so red so fast.

"I'm sorry. I know that must have been really hard for you." I felt so bad for him. Clearly he was holding back tears, probably because we were in public. *I wonder if he has talked to anyone about this. I wonder if Winter knows about it.*

"It's okay. What about you?" he asked, wiping away a tear and beginning to unfold the chicken wrap.

"What do you mean?"

"Tell me a little about yourself. Anything." With his bite of the chicken wrap, a ton of lettuce and bacon spilled onto the table. Furtively looking around, he tried to clean it up really fast. *He is so cute.*

"Well, as you already know, I have a younger sister, and we both live with our mom. We basically grew up here and know everyone in town." Never before had I been so cryptic in telling about my life, but I was trying to be careful not to mention Winter's name. I didn't want to talk about her. *Today isn't about her; it's about me.*

"What about your dad?"

"He and my mom got a divorce two years ago. So now he lives in Texas with his new happy family." The anger behind my sarcasm made me want to stab something.

"That sucks. How did you feel about that?" He placed both his arms against the table so that his clasped hands would be in the middle of it.

"I was angry. I actually still am." If I kept talking about this topic, then the reason I hated my dad would come out. I had never told anyone what really happened, other than my mother. It was not as if I could go to her for any emotional support. Maybe Liam could be the someone I had been looking for to fill that role.

"What did he do?" He seemed to want to know more, which I found a bit weird. I worried that if I told him what really happened that night, he might go on to tell Winter the truth about our parents' divorce.

"Can I trust you not to tell anyone?"

"You can trust me." He held out his little finger. "Pinky promise."

I held mine out as well, and we made the promise to each other. *Why is it that every time we touch, I feel as if I am being teleported to a cloudy day at the beach? I want to know what it means. Maybe I should visit a psychic on my next day off.*

"I caught my dad cheating on my mom with a very young woman." I look down immediately after saying that. *Why do I feel ashamed? Why does it feel as if I did something wrong?*

Liam reached for my hand and squeezed it tightly. Once I looked up, he immediately began to stroke my cheek with his other hand. Deep in my heart, this moment felt like home. When with him, I cared about no one else. It was as if time stopped as an image began to form in my mind. In it, we were running together at the beach on a cloudy, rainy day. Everything was gray and the ocean waves loud. The wind was blowing our hair away from our faces as we began to get closer to each other. *This feels too real to be a daydream. Oh, what I would do for it to be true!*

"It wasn't your fault." He said, his voice snapping me out of my reverie. "Your dad made a choice that hurt his family. He chose himself over his wife and daughters. He is the selfish one, not you. You

95

did the right thing by speaking up. You don't have to feel sorry about it." In a moment, he was looking straight into my eyes, still holding my hand and stroking my cheek. Then, in the next second, he was pulling away from me. "I'm sorry." His eyes began to wander to his phone and his surroundings.

Suddenly, the thought hit me: *He doesn't want to be seen with me.*

"It's fine," I said, "I need to leave, anyway." Grabbing my stuff, I headed out of the shop as quickly as I could. I pulled out my phone to call my mother to pick me up.

Just then I noticed how late it was. The sunset was so beautiful and bright. I loved it when the sky looked like cotton candy. That day, the clouds were a soft pink while the sky was a dark shade of blue. Being there at my favorite hour of day, after not seeing a sunset at the beach in so long brought me up short. *One day soon, exactly at the time the sun hides away from my face, I would go back.* There — at my happy place — I could let myself be at ease and truly content.

"At least can I take you home?" Liam said, standing right behind me — keys in hand.

"Why not…" I followed him to his car. It looked cleaner than the last time — smelling of pine trees and looking so shiny.

The entire ride home was extremely awkward. Neither of us knew what to say to the other. For a moment back at the coffee shop, I could see that he was clearly into me, but at this point, he was acting as if we'd never even met. I certainly didn't feel invited — or even allowed — to speak. *His thoughts and feelings must be in as much a muddle as mine. He probably thinks we got too carried away; and now, he feels sorry for me.*

It hurt, though. *No one places his hands on another person's cheek while they are looking into each other's eyes and then claims he doesn't feel anything. He's falling for me like I have been falling for him all along.* I wanted to know what was on his mind. His body was still as tense as it had been hours before. I didn't want to leave just then. I didn't want to let him go without questioning him, but I was so afraid of ruining everything.

"I'm sorry for what happened. I got carried away. I didn't mean to make you uncomfortable." He'd finally broken the silence of our drive to my house. Luckily, Winter was not home.

"It's fine," I said, looking down at the floor board. "You don't make me feel uncomfortable at all. I like being with you." Although I was trying to hide my nerves, my hands were shaking so badly that it felt as if I was about to play volleyball for the first time. *Is this what people mean when they talk about feeling butterflies in their stomach when they are in love?*

"I'm actually relieved to hear that. Will I see you tomorrow at school?" He hit the door locks so I could get out. It was getting late, and I didn't even know if he lived nearby. *I hope, he doesn't have to drive too far in the dark.*

"I'll see you there." I got out of the car and began to take a few steps toward my house. Something in my heart was telling me to go back, but at the same time I knew it was a bad idea to tell him how I felt. I'd promised not to date Liam. *Even if it kills me, I am still going to stick to my plan of avoiding Liam for the rest of the year. It's the right thing to do.*

Boys will come and go, but my sister is family. She will be with me for the rest of my

life.

Chapter 5

I have a love–hate relationship with dreaming at night about things that will never happen in real life. During my struggle with tangled relationships among Liam, Winter, and me; the dreams had been helping me escape from my reality and satisfy everything I wished I could do with the one I wanted to be with; the one I cared about the most. I just wished the dreams would last a bit longer. (Why did the alarm always have to go off at the most interesting and important part of the dream?) Each time the dream had felt so real. *But who am I kidding? The sad truth is that Liam and I will never be together. We were probably never meant to be together in the first place.* If he had been Winter's boyfriend at the time I first met him, I would not have allowed myself to feel anything for him. To me, it was a matter of honor to respect people's relationships, especially my sister's. What made it even more frustrating was for this conflict to happen the first time I had ever found someone attractive or that I cared to give my attention to. If only things had been different. Like most people, what I hated about such wonderful dreams was waking up to once again face that they were not real.

Out of all the places in the world I wanted to be, school was definitely not one of them. That week had been the busiest and most chaotic week of the semester so far. The juniors were making sure they finished putting up all the homecoming decorations while other people were planning and organizing parties for after the homecoming dance. My school was very strict about enforcing its policies during and after school activities. As far as I knew, homecoming had never been any exception. I thought it pathetic the way every year some people tried to sneak alcohol into the party even though everybody knew that the teachers would catch them the second they stepped into the gym. Not that I'd ever seen it happen; I had actually never been to a dance. I had never liked the idea of dancing with some strange dude I had just talked to for the first time. Plus, I had never been asked out by a guy and couldn't go with any of my friends since they always had dates to go with.

I wasn't intending to go that year, either. My mom had kept trying to convince me to go since it was my last year of high school. She said if I didn't, I'd end up regretting it later on; but she didn't seem to understand that going to a dance alone isn't any kind of fun. Since Winter would probably go with a date, I would be left on my own. *Of course, I would love to go with Liam, but we all know that is basically impossible. If I did, Winter would probably kill me in front of the whole school.* If not resorting to murder, at least she would have yelled at me and never spoken to me again. I just wanted that week to be over so that I didn't have to be reminded of it everywhere I looked on my way to classes.

For the project we had done together, Liam and I received the highest grade in the entire class. The two students who didn't show up to work on it with us got a zero for it, but I don't think they even cared. *How sad can that be? I wonder what's really going on with these kinds of students.*

Do they just have a lot going on at home, and the school hasn't reached out to them yet? Maybe, the school had already tried to help them, but the students didn't want to be helped. Maybe they thought it would require too much effort from them. *Was that the way I made my friends feel two years ago? Was that how I made my only best friend feel?*

Grace and I had been best friends since first grade. After my parents' divorce, she tried to be there for me as much as she could, but eventually she went away. Or rather, I pushed her away. I wasn't willing to talk to her or be with her, and she didn't force me to. As a result, I didn't only lose my dad; I lost my best friend, too, and it was all my fault. For almost two years, I hadn't even talked to Grace. I didn't even know much about her anymore. She did have a new best friend and a new boyfriend. *Just like the school has probably moved on from helping the troubled students, she has moved on without me.*

If I'd had the courage — I told myself — I would have done so many things. It's as if I'd made a list in my head: 1. I would make amends with Grace; 2. I would forgive my father for cheating on my

103

mom; 3. I would tell Winter the truth of what really happened with our parents; and 4. I would also tell her that I loved Liam. In a perfect world, telling the truth and doing the right thing would always be the easiest choice to make. However, this world is far from perfect. Certainly I, for one, was not perfect; but I had hope that one day, I would be brave enough to do all those things.

One day, I would have the courage to go after my dreams and after my dream guy. One day, I would be able to talk to my dad on the phone the way we used to talk in person every night at home. One day, I would be willing to meet my stepsiblings and my stepmother. One day, I would come to truly believe that much of what was happening to me happens to other people as well. *Until that day comes, I don't think I will ever change who I am. Why would I? If being brave is going to cause so much pain to others, why would I choose to be brave? If forgiving others is not going to take all of this pain and anger away, what is the point of it all?*

The only good thing about that week was that we didn't have class the next day because that night was the homecoming dance. The principal thought that dismissing classes would encourage more people to go to the dance since they could sleep in. Also, the girls would have plenty of time to get ready. A lot of people praised him for making that decision. I was just glad I didn't have to deal with all the mess for a fifth day that week.

And at least I don't have to deal with Winter tonight. That morning, she'd told mom that she was going to stay over at her friend's house so they could get ready together for the dance. Every year Winter went to the dance looking so beautiful. Sometimes I wished I was that beautiful — and with so little effort! Ever since Winter was a baby, we all knew she was going to be the cutest in the family. I'd never cared about it before, but that day all my focus was on yearning to be chosen by the only guy I had ever liked. *My beauty is nothing compared to Winter's. Liam will never choose me.*

"Hey, Summer," said a voice from behind me that I knew to be Liam's.

I had just been congratulating myself for making it to my car without incident. I really didn't want anyone to see me talking to Liam. Everyone at that school knew Winter. Plus, rumors always spread quickly among the popular kids. If anyone had seen Liam and me together, Winter would have known it in less than an hour.

"Hi," I said, throwing my backpack inside the car and closing the car door behind me. Liam had closed the distance between us and was standing so close to me that I could barely breathe. *I don't think he realizes how close he is.* My whole body was pressing against my car as I tried to put some inches between us. But those couple of inches were not enough. I needed space, and that afternoon was not the right time — and in front of almost the whole student body was not the right place — to talk to me.

"Are you going to go to the dance tomorrow?" he asked, looking at me both seriously and timidly as he took a step back. He began fidgeting his fingers while at the same trying not to act nervous.

Still, I knew exactly what he was going to ask me. Even though it was what I'd been wanting to happen all along, I also feared it.

"No, why?" I said, struggling to sound calm. I felt as if he was about to profess his love for me, and it hurt to know that I couldn't do the same, What's worse, I would have to lie to him so that I wouldn't end up hurting my sister. *Everything I want to do right now, is exactly the wrong thing.*

Immediately after my response, Liam turned around and began to walk in circles. I was touched that he felt he could show me his vulnerability, letting me see how scared and nervous he was. I felt so bad that the moment he would finally get up the courage to ask me to the dance, I would have to turn him down. *Hopefully, someday he will understand why I had to do it and forgive me.*

"Are you okay?" I asked him.

I longed for the agony to be over. Once I lied to him, he would go away and never speak to me again. *But is that what I really want?*

107

"Yes, I'm sorry. I don't know why I'm so nervous all of a sudden." Liam turned to face me. "I was wondering if you would like to go to the Homecoming dance with me. I know it's tomorrow, and you probably don't have anything to wear. If you want, we can go shopping together now or tomorrow morning. I can take care of everything, and if you don't want to go to the dance, we could go to the movies or do something else together instead, like a date," He paused for a split second and then rushed on. "That's if you want to. You don't have to if you're not interested. I'll be fine with either." His eyes were extremely wide. Both fear and excitement shone in them.

Of course, I wanted to say yes. I'd longed to go to the dance with him and was prepared to go shopping that very minute. I wanted to dance with him under the stars and look into his eyes as he held me close. I imagined that our foreheads would touch just seconds before his lips softly brushed mine. I would slowly intertwine my fingers with his, and we would kiss for seconds and then minutes. Out of my mouth would come the words I had never before said to anyone, and I would watch to catch my reflection in his eyes. I wanted to see the bright smile on his face and feel the warmth of his skin as I lay my head on his bare chest, listening to the resounding beat of his heart. Most of all, I wanted to have his all — and so much more — and for it to last forever. As everything I had always dreamed about flooded my thoughts, I deeply felt how unfair it was that none of those scenes would ever exist outside my mind.

"I'm sorry. I can't," I lied. "I have to work tomorrow."

"Maybe we could do something after?" he asked, sounding full of hope. "What time will you be off?"

"I don't think I'm going to be able to go after," I said hesitantly. "I'm sorry. I'm just going to be way too drained to do anything, and I don't want to end up being a burden." *I hate doing this. I don't want to lie to him. I don't even have to work tomorrow, but I also don't want him to think that I'm turning him down because I am not into him. What in the world should I say?* I didn't want to hurt his feelings, but if I didn't do it, I was going to end up hurting my sister.

"Maybe you can ask your manager to let you go early." Liam kept it up, seemingly trying to find solutions to the problem. *If only he knew the truth* ...

"I don't know. We're usually short-staffed on Fridays." I began to look at the ground because I couldn't stand it anymore. *I'm a horrible liar,* I thought, trying not to cry. *I feel like the most terrible person in the world.* Like my Dad, I was hurting the person I cared about most. *I'm just like my dad: a liar and a cheat.*

"That... sucks." Liam sighed, finally appearing to give up. He began to walk away from me but then stopped suddenly. "If you don't want to go with me, you can just tell me no." He turned his back to me but kept the same distance between us. "I know you don't work tomorrow because the place where you work is closed on Fridays."

"How — Wait, how do you know where I work?" I didn't recall telling him anything about my work life or posting about it on social media. *How could he know unless Winter told him?*

"It doesn't matter how I know, but what I don't know is why you are lying to me." Liam's face was red with frustration. He got closer to me and grabbed my hand, pressing his other hand against my car. As he leaned on me — his face and mine only about an inch apart — I could feel his warm breath on my skin.

"I just don't like you in that way, Liam." I pushed him aside so I could get my car door open and leave. I didn't want to prolong the misery of that conversation. And I really didn't want Winter or anyone else to see us arguing as if we were boyfriend and girlfriend.

"Don't you dare!" He slammed the car door closed again. "You are not leaving until we talk."

"Who are you, my dad?" I said, starting to get angry. He was being such a jerk. *It might seem like I deserved his reaction — if he didn't know full well why I'm doing this. He's just stubborn and wants to make me say it.*

"I am not a cheater," he said, loudly defending himself from ever being compared to my father. I could see in his eyes that he was hurt. Yet hurting him was the last thing I ever wanted to do. Ever since

111

the first time I saw him, I'd wanted to take care of him and protect him. I never would have thought that he would end up having to be protected from *me*.

"I know you dated my sister," I finally said.

I had been wanting to ask what happened between them, but I'd never thought it would have come about that way.

"Did she also tell you about all of those times she cheated on me?" Liam had moved to stand next to me. *I guess he's forgotten we're still in the school's parking lot.*

"She told me you caught her kissing another guy. That's all she said. She never mentioned anything else."

"That's it?" His laugh had an air of sarcasm to it. We both knew that this wasn't a joke; we were just tired of having to deal with the drama. I could see the weariness in his face which matched the irritation in his voice.

"Are you saying she cheated on you more than once?" I didn't even know if I should believe anything that he told me. *I've known*

Winter my whole life, and I met Liam less than two months ago. He could just be using me to get back at my sister.

"Never mind. I don't want to keep talking about her. She's your little sister; and clearly, you care about her. I'm not going to say anything to ruin your image of her." Placing himself in front of me, he held my chin so that I had to focus on him alone. "I know what you're doing. I knew it from the start. I just don't understand why we can't be together. Your sister never loved me, Summer. She never loved me the way I know you do."

"What? Liam, she still loves you, and you've got it all wrong." I said before he could see that I liked him and decide to lean in for a kiss. If we ever did kiss, I didn't want our first one to be intended only to prove that I was a better option than Winter. *I don't want to be an option. I want to be the only choice, someone he knows he can't live without.*

"Oh, cut the crap. Look, I don't know what she told you, but she clearly lied to you just like you're lying to me. Do you think I am so stupid that I would miss out on someone like you?" He let go of my

113

chin to grab the jangling phone from his pocket. "I have a doctor's appointment, so I have to go. Just promise me something, okay?"

"What?" I asked, not looking forward to his response.

"Come to the dance tomorrow."

"I —"

"You don't have to give me an answer. Just be there if you can, even if it is without me." He began to walk away so that I couldn't say anything back. I wished I could go. *I wish I didn't care so deeply about Winter's feelings, but that's who I am.*

"You know... just because someone says they love you, doesn't mean they really do." He said before immediately disappearing between cars.

What did he mean by that? *Winter is my sister, and she loves me as much as I love her.* I didn't have any doubts about that. She wasn't the kind of person to not love her sister back, and I had known plenty of other people that she also truly loved. She always had a lot of friends. *How can anyone have a lot of friends if they didn't show that they care about them?*

I don't think friendships can work without it. How could someone think she didn't care about any of her exes when I saw her cry after every breakup she ever had? And if she hadn't loved Liam, she wouldn't have felt sorry about hurting him.

Nothing was making any sense in my head. *How is it that I hate my father for cheating on my mom, but I go easy on Winter for the same thing? She deliberately cheated on Liam. It's that simple.* My sister knew what she was doing and that she would be hurting someone in the process. She betrayed Liam the way my dad betrayed us. *They're just alike. So, why have I been defending her all this time? Why would I justify her actions and even feel sorry for her?*

From the beginning I'd known what would happen, that one day the roles were going to be reversed, that Winter would become the heartbreaker and the guys the ones getting hurt. And when it did happen right in front of me with Liam, I'd been too naïve to see it. I just couldn't think of my sister as a monster. When I would look at her, I'd see the same little girl I used to take care of when we were little. I

115

couldn't just forget about how innocent and sweet she used to be, even if she made a horrible mistake.

No one changes completely. Somewhere in there that sweet little girl I knew was hiding. *She's just pretending to be hard-hearted because she's in pain and disappointed about everything that's happened.* I wanted her to feel safe and know that everything would be okay. I wanted her to stop wasting her time choosing all the wrong guys and then chasing after every one of them when he didn't love her anymore.

Can't she just have faith that love will find her at the right time? Can't she just wait patiently for The One? I want her to learn her lesson and move on to be a better person than she was with Liam If she doesn't, the perfect guy is going to just look away. No man wants to share the one he loves with someone else.

Chapter 6

I'd never before realized how quiet the house was when Winter wasn't around. I wondered if she was already getting ready for homecoming since it was only a couple of hours away. I still wished I was going to the dance too — but only with Liam. Even though he said he'd wait for me, I couldn't bring myself to get up from my bed. I'd been lying there since the day before, with nothing to eat or even a shower. *If only I could be at work right now, things would be so much easier on me.*

My mind was flooded with unwelcome thoughts. Never before had I been so indecisive about what to do. My heart was telling me to get up and meet Liam at the dance, but my brain was telling me

117

the opposite. I was too afraid to ask Winter if it would be okay to go to the dance with Liam. After all, only two months had passed since she'd confessed her intense love for him. *Maybe she's not in love with him anymore. Maybe she has finally moved on. I can't believe that I have no idea who she is going to the dance with.* No way would Winter go by herself, and I was sure she'd not started dating anyone again.

Liam had made it pretty clear that he didn't like Winter anymore. Probably, he still resented her for what she did to him — and who could blame him? I would be heartbroken if I'd caught the person I love kissing someone else. I could never imagine the gut-wrenching reaction he must have felt that day — not to mention the disappointment and anger that would linger for some time after.

It's so unfair that doing the right thing is in some ways also the wrong thing. By staying away from Liam, I was being a good, loyal sister; but it still felt so wrong. If life were fair, I should have been allowed to love the one I choose to love. But I stupidly chose to fall for the wrong guy. I couldn't see a way out of the situation without someone getting hurt. *How is it that my first love sounds like a page out of Shakespeare? If Liam and I start dating, Winter will never forgive me, but if Liam and I just deep our distance and ignore all of these chaotic and heavenly feelings, we will be torturing each other.*

It was only fair that I should have been able to freely express my feelings without any sense of guilt about it. *The only way that can have happen is for Winter to give her permission for us be together.* I hated how much control she had over us. On the other hand, I was the one who'd made the situation worse. I didn't have to fall in love so quickly and easily. *And I'm the one who isn't telling Winter the whole truth.*

Just then I heard what I thought was Winter's voice coming from the living room. *It's three o'clock in the afternoon. She should be at her friend's house getting her nails or hair ready.* At that point, I was so stressed about everything that I dreaded talking to her or even seeing her. *As long as she doesn't open my bedroom door and come in, everything will be just fine.*

Without a word, Winter burst through my bedroom door. Over her right shoulder was her homecoming dress in its fancy-dress bag. She was also struggling to carry her silver heels and make-up bag. She looked exhausted already, and it was nowhere close to seven o'clock.

In a matter of a couple of seconds, Winter had transformed my room to look like hers. I had never seen so much stuff in my life. Knowing that all of it was just for a homecoming dance made me feel poor. Winter had brought the entire store with her. I wondered how she could afford all those different kinds of jewelry, make up, and hair stuff. *I don't even own a simple tube of lip gloss or a bracelet.* But I wasn't really concerned about that. What actually concerned me was how I was going to get out of that situation and what my life was going to look like the rest of the afternoon.

"So, it turns out that getting ready with a lot of girls is not as fun as it sounds," Winter said, after the moving job was done. "In minutes we had run out of space since everyone had to dress and to wash hair and to shave to be ready for tonight. So, I'm getting ready here instead."

That sounded really ominous to me. That much time together brought with it so much risk since with every word I got dangerously close to what I dreaded.

Too quickly I had to change my plan of action. After all, my wishes had been completely denied, and at this point, I had no other options than to face my fears. I didn't think I had enough energy left to pull off just pretending that everything was fine with me. Besides, I really wanted her to know how I felt about Liam and that I wasn't interested in competing with her to be with him. Winter was in the dark about all the times Liam, and I had met after school or, more important, that he had feelings for me.

"I hope you don't mind helping me since I know you're not going" Winter said, in the wake of my silence. Sitting on the floor close to the mirror, she began to pull out different kinds of makeup products.

"That's fine. What do you need help with?"

"Can you do my makeup?" she asked, turning around to give me her puppy eyes. She knew that even though I hated doing makeup or even wearing it, somehow, I was pretty good at doing *her* makeup.

"Sure, I guess." I had to walk around all her stuff to sit next to her on the floor. "What color are you wearing?"

"Dark blue. It complements my eyes," she said, showing off her ocean-blue eyes to me as if I had never seen them before.

"Do you have any ideas about what you want?"

"Yes." In the picture on her phone the eyeshadow was blue with glitter in the middle, silver closest to the nose, and black on the outside. All the colors were blended so well that it looked unreal. I had never done such a complicated makeup look. *I hope it turns out okay. I'm not in the mood to get yelled at for the next couple of hours.*

"You know, that looks a little bit complicated." I really wanted to do something simple. After all, with her face, she would have been fine with just lipstick, mascara, and a little bit of blush. I never understood why she always wanted to wear so much makeup.

"I know. That is why I want you to do it." She flashed me a smile and reached for an eyeshadow palette and makeup from her bag.

"Okay. Don't open your eyes until I'm done."

It might have taken me thirty minutes to finish one eye, but I was impressed with the results.

"You want to see how it looks before I start with the other eye?" I asked.

She answered by quickly moving closer to the mirror. "Summer, it looks so good. Omg! Thank you so much! You are the best sister ever!" Winter gave me a quick hug and then went back to the mirror to analyze every little detail of the makeup masterpiece.

This is good. She is happy, and I am happy for her. That's all that matters. That is all we need.

"Can you do my hair when you're done with my makeup?" She said, moving to cozy up next to me again.

"Yeah, I guess."

Why is it always me helping Winter get ready and not mom? I thought all moms would be happy to do that kind of thing with their daughters. Instead, she was in the living room watching TV and probably scrolling down through social media. *Why can't she at least be here talking to us?* I tried to recall any mother-daughter memory like the ones I had with my dad. Then I stopped. I didn't want to get anywhere near any of the memories I had with my dad. Why couldn't I have a great relationship with mom and not him? Winter and I deserved that. We had needed her so many times, but even though she was there physically, her role in our lives was more as a spectator than an active player.

After about two hours, Winter was almost ready to go. She was leaving early so she could meet her friends to take pictures before the dance. At the mention of pictures, I once again regretted that she'd chosen such heavy makeup when the lighter and simpler makeup style would have looked so much better for pictures. I did feel pleased that she liked it, though.

"I kind of wish you were going to the dance," Winter said, carefully taking off her clothes so as not to ruin her curly hair.

"I was thinking about going, but it's too late now." I sat down on my bed and tried to not stare at her as she changed into her blue dress.

"Really? Did you have a date?"

"No. By the way, who are you going with?"

"I'm going with this new guy from my history class. I don't think you know him, but he's just really hot." After adjusting her dress, she sat next to me to put on her silver heels.

The thought just hit me that Winter looked exactly like Cinderella. Her naturally blonde straight hair had been transformed into bouncy curls like mine. Her blue ocean eyes shone as bright as they could be. She looked perfect in every way a person could. Even with all that makeup, her skin looked flawless. In her blue, short, puffy dress, she was a princess awaiting her Prince Charming. Maybe for once, this new prince wouldn't break her heart. For the hundredth time, I asked myself, *How could anyone ever hurt such an ethereal being?*

"Why are you looking at me like that?" Winter asked, her face filled with confusion and embarrassment. *Deep down in her heart she knows how I'm feeling right now. She knows exactly why, too. She's always been able to read me like a book.*

"You look beautiful. I kind of wish dad was here." *I can't believe I just said that out loud. I don't want her to think I miss dad being around.* At times I couldn't help but think about how important it is for a teenage girl to have a father figure. *Aren't dads supposed to set the bar high so that no childish boy can catch his girl's attention? No wonder Winter has terrible judgment about men — and why she doesn't know how to treat them either.*

"I know." Winter glanced at the wall where all of my family pictures were hanging — including many pictures of Winter and me throughout the years of our life together. Since day one, we'd looked nothing alike. After everything that had happened, I was relieved to look more like our mother than our father. *At least I won't be reminded of*

126

him for the rest of my life every time I look at myself in the mirror. I wondered how Winter would feel when she found out the truth about him. *Is she going to hate him the way I do? Or would she forgive him as if it's nothing? Would she even be upset or mad at him?* Thinking about that secret I'd been keeping from her made my mind turn to another way I'd been lying by keeping the truth from her.

"I have to talk to you about something." I knew it was probably not the best time for it. *But if not now, then when?*

"What? Is it about Liam?" Winter said, turning toward me.

"Yes. Did you ever get a chance to talk to him?" I sounded more nervous than I'd thought I would be. The look on her face told me that she knew how I was feeling. I guess the fact that I nearly ran out of breath to complete that one question had tipped her off.

"No. I think he blocked me a while ago. Why?" She started rummaging through her jewelry box to pick out a couple of sets of silver earrings, a few bracelets, and her favorite necklace.

"Oh, I was just wondering." Her words had sent a sensation of relief rushing through my body. My suspicions about Liam's intentions toward me had been wrong. All of my worries were slowly starting to disappear. Finally, I am the one being chosen!

"Summer…" Winter said as she struggled with the clasp of her diamond necklace.

"What?" I said, already knowing her reply. I had been waiting for that moment for a long time and still didn't know whether or not I should tell the truth.

"Do you like him?" Even though Winter was not looking at me, she seemed a bit too annoyed and nervous to really be comparing the two different pairs of earrings she held.

I never thought she would just blurt out that question. *Now's my chance to tell her the truth instead of wondering if she already knows it. How can I keep lying to my little sister?* I had been feeling awful about it. Plus, I didn't think myself capable of lying directly to her face. *I should always tell the truth, no matter how much pain it will cause to someone else. Isn't that the*

128

ethical thing to do? Besides, what if she later finds out from someone else? I don't want her to hate me. I don't want her to feel betrayed. I don't want her to feel the way I felt when I saw dad being with another woman. I am better than he is. I had no doubts about that.

"Winter, I —"

"Please, don't lie to me." Winter moved closer to me on the bed. Her eyes were starting to get watery and her face full of a worry that I had never seen there before. I hated to be the one causing it, but my heart was directing me to tell her the truth no matter what. *Anyway, it's too late to back down. She already knows the answer without me having to say it.*

"I do . . . like him." Thinking about it had been so dreadful, but finally admitting it out loud felt wonderful. It was as if a ton of weight had been lifted off my shoulders. I felt more than free. I felt as if I was no longer in hiding.

"When did this start?" Winter said, throwing a pair of earrings on the floor. She turned around too quickly for me to tell if she was mad or just didn't like that pair.

"Since I first saw him at the mall. I didn't know he was the boy from your camp. I promise that if I knew, I would not have let myself like him. That's why I asked you about him, but you pretended that you didn't see him there. What was I supposed to do?" I felt as if all the oxygen had just left my body, to be replaced by a kind of adrenaline I'd never felt before. At the time, I didn't think I ever wanted to feel it again.

"Why didn't you tell me when I told you what had happened at the camp?" Winter sounded frustrated. I didn't blame her. She was right. I should have told her how I felt that day. I should have not assumed she already knew.

"I thought you knew! You basically implied that he was off limits. I just figured you already knew I had started liking him." The mixture of feelings in this room was so toxic. *With us both playing the victim, I don't see this conversation going anywhere any time soon.*

"That doesn't mean anything! You should have told me. You should have stopped talking to him instead of hanging out with him after school and lying to me for months. Did you really think I wouldn't notice? Did you really think I wasn't going to find out about it? People talk, Summer. I have heard everything from everyone — except you." Winter began to pick up her stuff and hurry toward the door.

"You are not leaving until we talk. You've got it all wrong." I said, grabbing her arm to yank her back into my room. "We only hung out once because we were working on a school project together. Ask our teacher — or do whatever if you don't believe me. Don't you dare think for one minute that I tried to be with Liam after you told me you still love him. I care about you more than anyone else in this world, Winter. You are my sister. For your sake I went out of my way to avoid him. He means nothing to me. I would —"

"Then why do you still like him?" She screamed, at the top of her lungs. *She doesn't want to listen. She has already set her mind on believing that I am the monster and she the innocent one.*

"You are not being fair at all, Winter."

"How am I not being fair? He was my boyfriend. I loved him first! You are just the second one in line." She pushed me out of the way and ran down the hall to her room.

"You didn't care about Liam! You cheated on him!" I ran after her and threw open her bedroom door.

The moment the words left my mouth, I knew what was going to happen. I just never thought it would have happened that day out of all days.

"Go to hell, Summer." Winter yelled as her hand hit me across my left cheek.

For a couple of seconds, we both stood paralyzed, seeming to have no reactions to what just happened. I wasn't sure about Winter, but I was too scared to say anything else that could have made the whole situation worse.

How could Winter ever lay a hand on me when all I've ever done is taken such great care of her? Pain and disappointment overwhelmed me. *How did my sweet Winter become this type of person?* I guess I'd been too naïve to notice that my little sister had been growing into a very different girl from the one I used to know.

"My friends are outside. I'm leaving." She put her phone in her sparkly purse and headed out of her bedroom. Seconds later, she walked back in to find me exactly the way she'd left me. "If you show up at the dance, I will never speak to you again." Then she slammed the door so hard that I could feel the vibration from the floor to the bottoms of my feet.

First, she refuses to listen to me. Second, she refuses to understand my side of the story. Then, she demands me to stay away from her and from Liam as if Liam is her property, and she can do whatever she wants with him. After everything she made him go through, did she really think he'd ever give her another chance? I hoped not because she certainly didn't deserve it. *She probably doesn't even like him anymore. What about the guy she is going to the dance with? Is she just using him to get back at Liam? Is she going to try to make him jealous?*

I concluded that my sister was just like our dad — so selfish that she couldn't, for one second, care about my feelings or anyone else's for that matter. After everything, I still believed that the thing with Liam didn't have to tear us apart. *Why can't she understand that I was willing to do anything to make her happy?* I was always willing to ignore how I felt to protect her at all costs. I never intended to hurt her. I hadn't planned to fall in love with Liam. *Why won't she believe me?*

134

Chapter 7

Will I ever be anyone's special someone? I wondered, as I still sat — numb — on Winter's bed. *If that day ever comes, and I'm still young, I will play hide and seek with my lover.* I wanted to hold hands as we made our way to the beach to watch the sunrise. I wanted to intertwine our arms whenever we had to walk into strange places that made us feel uncomfortable. On a hot summer day, we would hold pinkies as we walked down the street, eating ice cream. I could see myself resting my head on his chest after a long day at work as we both fell asleep to a movie. In my dreams of the future, I was smiling proudly as I listened to him talk for hours about things he was interested in.

I wanted to fall asleep with goodnight kisses and cuddles after talking about how much we missed each other during the day. I wanted to wake up to watch him, still asleep, breathing so slowly and peacefully next to me. I would bake a cake for his birthday and make sure he relived his happy memories from childhood. We could share kisses underwater, under the rain, under the snow, under the blankets, and under the stars. I wanted to share a wholesome moment by lying in the middle of a wildflower field while telling stories about our childhood. We'd go on long drives and listen to the songs we both loved.

My plans were so detailed that they included all the holidays that were important to me. At Halloween, we would carve pumpkins and have arguments about which one was best. On Thanksgiving night, I wanted to start decorating the Christmas tree; knowing we would be too sleepy to finish. On New Years' Eve we would dance all night long under the sky as fireworks lit up the sky. I wanted to receive flowers and chocolates on Valentine's and every day before and after that. In short, my dream was to make memories we could look back on when we were too old to remember anything else. And at least we would remember each other because we'd fully had each other for a lifetime.

That last, all-encompassing joy I wished for Winter as well. *Surely everyone feels this way. Don't people want the same things?* To me, the challenge was that you had to find someone who was willing to give you their all at the same time you are giving them your all. I saw this as the only way to find true, everlasting love and not get hurt. Winter didn't give her all when she was with Liam while Liam gave her all he could. If I had been Winter, I would have given him everything I could. I never would have broken his heart by betraying him. *How does she not understand that people can't trust easily after someone hurts them so deeply?* I could only hope that in the future she would find someone she could be willing to give herself to completely.

Why doesn't she value my feelings for Liam? Does she think I don't truly love him? Maybe if she had asked me about it, she would have noticed how serious my feelings were and wouldn't have tried to get him back. All sorts of worst-case scenarios kept bubbling up in my mind. *What if all this is just an obsession of hers? What if Liam does give her another chance, and she hurts him again?* I didn't want to sit there — in *her* room — and do nothing about it. I wanted to profess my love to Liam the way I should have two months before. *However, is it really worth it?* came the question that always held me back. *Will ruining my relationship with my sister be worth it just so I can be with the first person I have ever wanted and loved?*

As I began walking back toward my room, I noticed my mother standing at the end of the hallway. She was looking straight at me with zero emotions, so I hadn't any idea about what she was up to. Probably, she just heard Winter and me arguing and was curious.

While I was pushing my bedroom door to close it, my mom was moving to prevent it from closing and then came in right behind me.

"What were you two arguing about?" Mom asked while making her way to the side of my bed.

"A lot." I had never talked to her about boys before. But then Winter and I had never argued before, either. Probably, I would have to tell her everything that had been going on since the beginning of the school year, and I wasn't sure how.

"Are you going to the dance?" she asked, the question's seeming to come out of nowhere.

But I could see through her ploy. She already knew I didn't like going to those things so just wanted to deflect to another topic to hide her curiosity — and from her own daughter.

"No."

Can't she just get to the point? Didn't she realize that this was her chance to finally give me some advice? *If she doesn't hurry, it will be too late. I will never make it to the dance on time.* I had no expectations from her, but if her advice seemed good enough, I was prepared to reconsider my decision.

"Look, I'm sorry for being too busy and tired all the time to check on you two more often, but I do know that you two never fight like this. So, tell me. What's going on?"

139

She inspected my room from top to bottom as if she had never been there before. It had easily been months or maybe even a year since she'd come into my room. I wondered if she was surprised that it hadn't changed at all.

"Did Winter tell you about the guy she dated during the summer?" I said, grudgingly, since I didn't want to talk about Winter. If I told mom things she hadn't, Winter would hate me even more.

"Liam?"

"Yes, did she tell you what happened between them?"

"Winter got caught cheating on him, so he broke up with her," she said. I was surprised that she knew that much. Since she'd never talked about it, I was left to wonder whether or not she had any idea about what was going on. "Didn't he start to go to your school?" she asked, staring at me, as she waited patiently for my response.

"He did. He's actually in my grade. We have a couple of classes together." I zoned out for a few seconds and woke to realize how distant I felt from my own mother. It was as if I was talking to a complete stranger.

"You like him, don't you?" she said pinching my left cheek and making a silly face. I felt so embarrassed that I was afraid I would throw up on my bed.

"How do you know these things?" I was blushing for a lot of reasons, but mainly because someone finally seemed to accept how I felt toward Liam and also that I would have the chance to let that out.

"I could see a little spark in your eyes just then. So, tell me, does Liam like you back?" She moved closer to the end of my bed to be able to lean back on the wall. She looked so tired. The bags under her eyes had been getting more noticeable ever since she'd started working night shifts on top of her day shifts at the hospital. I felt bad for her. She hadn't deserved to be left alone with two teenaged daughters.

"He does, but it's complicated." I moved back to lean against the wall beside her. It seemed that this time together was going to be

141

longer than I would ever have expected. *I might end up not going to the dance after all.*

"How so?" My mom said as she reached over to sweep my dark curly hair out of my eyes.

"Winter says she still loves him."

"I see…" She looked down for a couple of seconds. I imagined she must have been thinking that no matter what she advised me to do, one of her daughters was going to end up getting hurt. "Can you tell me exactly what has been going on? I really do want to give you the best advice. I love both of you girls so much. I know I don't show it all the time, but I want to help."

"It's fine, mom." I started at the beginning and told her just about every detail of what had happened. "With what I found out after doing a little research on social media, I knew I couldn't like him because Winter would get so mad at me for it. I really did try, mom, but as much as I tried to stay away from him, I always seemed to find myself in a situation with just the two of us. I really do like him, mom. I have never felt this way before about anyone. Ever since dad left, I have seen all boys as my number one enemy. I have been so afraid of getting hurt the same way you got hurt. I didn't want to fall in love, and I've never been in love until now. Why does it have to be with the one person I can't have? What makes him so special?" My flood of words matched the flood of emotions I had kept inside for two years, not willing to share them with anyone.

Before I knew it, I found my head in her lap. By the time I finished my last sentence, I was in tears. I hadn't cried next to my mom since I was a little kid. I felt so confused and exhausted. Not being able to talk to someone about my true feelings had been deteriorating every single piece of my beating heart.

"I don't understand, Summer. Why do you think you can't be with Liam? From what it sounds like, Liam doesn't want to give your sister another chance, anyway." She was playing with my hair with one hand and with the other rubbing my back. A sense of calm and deep comfort settled into me.

"She told me that she is still in love with him and that even if I just show up at the dance, she will never speak to me again." I am crying all over Mom's nicest pair of light blue jeans.

"Summer, you two are sisters. You will have to deal with each other, one way or the other, for the rest of your lives. Right now, Winter is being selfish. But eventually she will realize that none of this is a good enough reason to never talk to you again." She brought me up closer to her so that the side of my face was pressing against her right shoulder.

"I want you to understand something," she went on. "We can't control who we love and who we don't. When it's someone we shouldn't love, we just have to pretend to not like them until those feelings go away. Now, are you absolutely sure that your love for this guy is greater than anything you can imagine in the world? Are you willing to make hard sacrifices to be with him knowing that at times he may hurt or betray you?"

I had never thought about love that way. She made it sound like the most magical feeling a person could ever have, but she also made it sound like the worst curse that could ever befall any human being. So I was confused about how to answer her. *Am I ready to give myself to Liam? Am I willing to love him more than anyone else, to put him before my own needs and wants?* And the scariest question of all: was I willing to run the chance of getting my heart shattered like a blown-glass figurine.

"Mom, I know I love Liam." As I turned toward my mother, I realized I was staring at her with the most serious look I had given her since I told her about dad. In that moment I made up my mind about what to do. *No one can stop me, not even Winter. Not even my sister.*

"Then what are you waiting for? Let's get you ready for the dance." Before I could think twice, my mom had jumped up to run out of my room and down the hallway.

The truth of my relationship with Winter became suddenly clear. All that time, while I was berating myself for wanting the same person she wanted, I had in my mind an image of Winter as my beautiful, innocent sister who deserved to have the whole world. And all that time, she was manipulating me. She saw me as the perfect tool to help her obtain the only guy who'd had enough of her. I was coming to see that Winter never really loved him and didn't really love me either, at least not in the way I'd thought. If she'd really cared about me, she wouldn't ever have threatened to end our relationship if I came between her and Liam. *He doesn't belong to her just like he doesn't belong to me. He is not a possession. He is a human being just like us. He already made his choice, and Liam chose me. This is my moment. This is my opportunity to experience the wild, beautiful, chaotic, and exotic love that everyone should get to experience at least once in a lifetime.*

Chapter 8

I don't think I'd ever felt so anxious. The knot in my throat wouldn't go away, and the pounding in my chest was so fast and so forceful that I could feel and see my heartbeat through the silky red dress I was wearing. My breathing had almost reached the level of hyperventilating. No one had ever come up with a kind of breathing technique that could help me during such times. In this case, I was too overwhelmed by the threat that Winter had delivered only a few hours before.

Why can't I just be spontaneous and reckless like Winter? Aren't I allowed to be madly in love with someone? Why do I have to care so much about hurting my sister? No one had ever cared as much about me as Liam did.

Looking at the contrast between the two, I felt stupid for thinking that Winter cared about me one little bit. Even so, the more I thought about it, the more I wanted to turn around and go back home. As I imagined Winter's face and possible reaction toward my rebellion against her, I wanted to just disappear into an unknown place.

I had been sitting in the parking lot for the past twenty minutes — better known as the longest twenty minutes of my life. Since I hadn't seen a single soul in that time, I assumed that everyone else had already arrived. The sounds from the gym — of people screaming, singing, laughing, and talking — reminded me of how much I wished I had friends to support and encourage me.

I didn't even feel like myself. I had never been decked out in such a fancy way. My hair was pulled up in a soft, long braid with a red satin ribbon tied at each end. My mom had applied my makeup exactly the way I directed — perfectly accented with a light amount of blush, mascara, eyeliner, and a bit of light brown eyeshadow. She had made me wear her red lipstick even though I tried millions of times to convince her not to. I'd always liked lighter, neutral colors. But my mom was so enthusiastic for me to wear her ancient prom dress from high school, and the lipstick matched it perfectly. Even though it was outdated, it was also the most beautiful, elegant, and sexy dress I had ever owned — or even seen, for that matter. The dress was floor length with a slit up the right leg.

"Be careful to move and step cautiously," my mother thoughtfully warned me, "that is, if I you don't want to show the crowd a whole lot more than thigh!" The A-Line silhouette fit perfectly around my small chest, as if it was made for me.

I thought it strange that I had never seen the dress before — and even stranger that it was still intact after all those years. That made me wonder what my mom looked like in it. Then, in turn, I felt bad for not wanting to get to know my mom and for treating her so harshly. I would often forget about all of the things she had gone through. *She's probably been feeling lonelier than I have. I can't wait for tonight to be over so that I can give her the longest hug in the world. She deserves it.*

149

"Summer, is that you?" A girl said from right next to my car window.

I jumped so high that the top of my head slammed up against the roof. *Ouch! Hitting cars is more painful than hitting a wall. How can someone be here when I haven't seen anyone go into or come out of the gym for the past half an hour?*

"I am so sorry, Summer." she said, bending down to peer in at me. "I shouldn't have just come up behind your car. I didn't mean to scare you,"

It was my long-lost best friend, Grace. The post light beaming on her face revealed makeup similar to what I did for Winter. Form fitting and glittery, her red dress was nothing like the one I had on. I couldn't even recall the last time we spoke to each other or even what it was about. *I hope she doesn't hate me for not talking to her the way I used to. Maybe she is my answer or the aid to my problems. For sure, she is exactly what I need right now.*

After a couple of seconds of contemplation, I decided to open the door and get out, hoping against hope that she would be willing to enter the dance the with me.

"Why were you sitting in your car?" She asked. I was looking at the ground, scared and anxious about what to do next. I didn't want to bother her with all my problems, supposing that she had a lot going on in her life as well. *I wonder how many times I wasn't there to help her with something. I am such a terrible friend. I am such a terrible daughter as well. I am such a horrible sister.*

"What's wrong?" Grace added. "I know we haven't talked in a while, but you can still talk to me about anything,"

Looking into her eyes, I felt even more guilty for how I'd pushed her away. She was just trying to be there for me, like any good friend. As I stood next to Grace in that parking lot, I couldn't fathom how, back then, I seemed to blame her for everything that was happening to me — and more: for not understanding how I was

151

feeling, for not making all the pain and anger go away, for not being able to make my life better.

"I am not mad at you," Grace said, filling up the dead silence from me. "I knew you needed space after your parents' divorce. I really hoped you were going to find your way back to me. After all, we were best friends… I am really sorry for not trying harder to be there for you." She moved toward me and pulled me close for a quick hug. I hadn't felt close to anyone in such a long time. As much as I'd tried to have a meaningful and deep relationship with my little sister, all she seemed to want for me was to be unhappy.

"It was not your fault, Grace. I shut you out. I know you tried to be there for me. I am the one who should be apologizing, not you." I began to tear up. I was sniffing so badly that I expected that my nose was turning red.

"Well, are we cool, then?" Grace asked.

"Yes, we are cool." I leaned over to give her another quick hug, but she stopped me before I could reach my arms behind her back.

"Do you really think I've forgotten my original question? Why were you sitting in your car?" She crossed her arms and frowned.

"It's a long story. I can tell you later." As I grabbed her arm to start walking toward the gym, something stopped me as if I'd hit a wall. Grace had become a dead weight, refusing to move until I told her what was going on. I missed that. I missed having her in my life even if sometimes her personality was to be a pain in the butt. "Fine. What do you want to know?"

"Everything. I haven't talked to you in two years. I want to know what's going on in your life."

Seeing that she was moving side to side in to get warm, I suggested we talk in the car.

Even in the car, it was so cold that I could see her exhaled breath. As for me, I was too cold to move my body — even my fingers.

153

I'd lost the feeling in my fingers and toes a couple of minutes before we got into the car.

"So . . ." Grace drew out the word as she waved her cold hands in front of the air vents.

"I met a guy and his na-"

"You met a guy?" She burst out in total shock. She reached out to pull me close. With our faces only a few inches apart, she was staring directly into my eyes. Slowly spreading across her face was an awfully weird, huge smile that could mean so many different things. "I'm sorry. I just don't think I've ever heard those words come out of your mouth. I have been waiting for this moment for, like, a decade."

"First, you are exaggerating," I said, pushing her away as I lay back against the door.

"I am definitely not." She leaned closer to me seeming determined to win her unimportant, little argument.

"Do you want to know what is going on or not?" I asked her, annoyed.

154

Grace loved the satisfaction of always being right, but for me, that was the most insignificant part of our conversation. Actually, that day I didn't mind that much because it was so vintage Grace — the sometimes weird and silly best friend I'd known for so long. For me, the satisfaction was seeing that she hadn't changed that much after all.

"Okay. Go on." She lay back on her side, offering me her sad-puppy face. Even with that makeup on, she still somehow managed to look like a little kid. *No wonder her parents go easy on her.*

Finally I had what I had been needing so badly: someone who was not friends with Winter so I could talk to her about everything that had been going on and then she could give me an honest opinion about my sister.

I poured out to her what been going on from the end of summer to the present. I emphasized the way Winter and Liam ended their relationship and that Liam didn't like her anymore because of it. I made sure Grace knew that as soon as I found out who Liam really was, I stopped talking to him as much as I could even if it was torturous for me. Of course she had to know that Winter had made it clear to me that I couldn't date him. Best of all, I felt free to tell Grace everything I couldn't tell my mom because I didn't want to put my mom in the middle, where she might have had to choose between her two daughters.

"Okay, So, let me get this straight. Winter cheated on this guy, and now this guy likes you and you like him, but you can't be together because Winter doesn't want you to?" Grace said, her tone a mixture of confusion and annoyance.

"Yes." I said, a bit sheepish since the straightforward way she'd put it had made the whole situation sound kind of stupid.

"Summer, I know Winter is your sister, but have you ever heard what people say about her at school?" Grace readjusted herself, pulled her phone out of her small silver purse, and looked at me for a response.

"No, why?" I asked, so naively. I'd always been confident that I knew my sister, but after recent events, I was unsure of anything having to do with Winter.

"You know that she has a reputation with boys, right?" Grace said, unlocking her phone and starting to search it.

"I know she has dated a lot of people. The only thing she has ever told me is that those guys treated her like trash, and that is why she ended up breaking up with them." I tried to search my mind for any time I'd ever heard Winter give a different explanation after a break up, but was sure that she had repeated the same speech ever since her first boyfriend cheated on her.

"Summer, she is lying to you." Grace gave me a serious look and handed me her phone.

"What is this?" I asked vaguely.

"My friends have been sharing these screenshots on a group chat for the past couple of weeks. I think you should look at them," she responded while moving behind me to look over my shoulder.

I held Grace's phone and read all of the screenshots of Winter's texts to various guys. In them, she wasn't just flirting but also sending them inappropriate pictures of herself with barely any clothes on. Some of the text messages were from a week ago and some from the current week as well. The screenshots were shared by some guys on the football team, and the guys Winter was talking to had been football players as well.

Worse was the gossip about Winter on this particular group chat I was not even familiar with. Some of the postings were calling her names and commenting on her body in ways I would have preferred never to read about. It was so painful and disappointing. I was angry at so many things, but the damage was already done. I could do nothing about it.

I hadn't expected Winter to stay a sweet young girl forever; I just naively thought that when she left childhood, she would grow into a good person with some innocence still left in her. *How did I not see this coming? Am I that self-absorbed to not notice what was happening right next to me?*

"I'm sorry that you had to find out so late about all of the stupid things she's been doing. Probably I should have told you sooner so you could've kept her from making so many careless decisions. Also, I thought if you knew the truth, you'd realize that it isn't your responsibility to protect Winter where boys are concerned. Think about it; she's probably been lying to you about still having feelings for this guy. How can she possibly love him that much if she is entertaining other guys?"

"Why would she lie to me like that?"

"Maybe you made her mad without even realizing it," Grace answered, reaching for her phone to put it back into her purse.

I wracked my brain to come up with anything I'd done to hurt my sister. *Could it be that Winter knew all along or just found out about what our dad did to our mom? Even so, that doesn't explain why she would be mad at me. I wasn't the one who hurt mom.*

159

"I don't know..." I said, looking straight at the gym entrance.

"Either way, Winter is being really unfair and selfish about all this. You have to understand that you are not doing anything wrong. Nothing is going on between that guy and Winter anymore because your sister lied and hurt him. It's not your fault you fell for him. Summer, you can't go on pleasing your little sister for the rest of your life. I know you've always cared about her, and it's not fair that your sister doesn't care the same way about you."

Deep down, I knew this. It was just hard to take in the fact that the person you cherished the most wanted to make sure you were miserable in every possible way. I was beginning to see that I was the only one who could stop Winter. If I didn't, she was going to keep doing this to me, or mom, or someone else. All I ever wanted was for us to be closer to each other. I'd hoped we'd be the kind of sisters who are best friends as well. *How can I be friends with someone who lies to me, manipulates me, and wants to control my every move from where I go, to who I fall in love with? That is not what a friend does. These are the actions of someone who doesn't like you or hates you. And Winter is not just my friend. She's my sister.*

"Okay," I said, shutting off the car engine and with it the heater.

"Okay? What do you mean 'okay'?" A smile was trying to dispel the confusion on her face, but something seemed to be stop her from completely showing off how pleased she was.

"I am going to go in there and tell Liam that I love him," I said — so confidently that adrenaline shivers overcame my entire body.

"That's my girl!" She said, offering her hand for a high-five.

After the high-five, we burst out laughing — mostly because we simultaneously realized that after thirty minutes in the car, we'd missed most of the dance. We got out of the car so quickly that Grace dropped her purse twice. That began our comedy routine of racing across the parking lot to the gym to arrive just in time to fulfill my love fantasy. All the while, I was trying to silence my mom's warning me about the dress. That had become the least of my worries.

161

I bet I look utterly crazy right now. — *my curls bouncing from side to side while I'm trying to make tracks in three-inch heels that are threatening to break any minute.* By the time we reached the door, I was so out of breath that I doubted that I had the strength to come up with the right words to tell Liam about how much I had thought of him since the first day we met. *But even if everything goes to hell after tonight, this moment is all I ever could have wished for. I have my mother's support, and best of all, I have won back what I lost two years ago: my best friend.*

Chapter 9

I was amazed to see the number of people still there. But then again, the parties wouldn't begin until midnight.

As I scoured the room among the many faces I spotted and recognized, I was relieved that Winter was nowhere to be found. I doubted that she'd already gone home, because she wouldn't want to miss any of the after parties. She liked going to events where she could have fun without any parental supervision. *Wait a minute, Winter could be in the bathroom or just hiding somewhere, making out with her date. That sounds like her... Doesn't it?* It felt so bizarre to think that of my sister.

I had always known that Winter was popular. But I also naively believed that she wasn't like all the other girls I'd heard about. I

163

wanted to believe that my little sister had a sense of self-respect and dignity. But I was coming to realize that Winter was not as happy as she made out to be. She would be so friendly and always wanted to be surrounded by people, to hang out with someone or go out in groups. She didn't ever allow herself to be alone.

Sadly, I don't think she knows how. That's really bad because the only way she can learn about herself is when she's alone. She needed time to think and process her actions and mistakes, to focus on what matters in life instead of what was keeping her behind. *How can she not see that following what everybody is doing is only going to get her into more trouble, and worse, trash her reputation? I wouldn't be surprised if when she finds the perfect guy, he ends up running away after hearing everything she did as a teenager. Why would any man want to be with someone who jumps from one relationship to another? Why would someone want a woman who let just anyone have her? Why would he want to kiss lips that have been kissed by more people than he could count?* I wouldn't blame the perfect guy for ending up reconsidering his feelings toward Winter. No one wants to be anxious and fearful throughout a relationship. Isn't trust one of the most important requirements between two people who love each other? How can anyone love someone who clearly is not trustworthy?

As for me — I was at ease knowing that I would give myself completely to Liam and that he would do the same back. How lucky could I be? He was all I ever dreamed of when I was a little kid. I loved knowing that our feelings for each other were mutual — that is, if he hadn't changed his mind. Since I was really late for the dance, I could only hope that he hadn't given up on me. I was determined not to end up shattering his pure heart the way Winter did. His heart deserved to be whole again.

Although I was happy Winter wasn't there, I was scared that I didn't see Liam anywhere either. *I will never forgive myself if he thinks I've abandoned him. How can I sleep tonight without seeing him first?* I didn't care if I had to find my way to his house — even if it took all night. I vowed to tell him how I felt before sunrise. *Tomorrow might be too late. I refuse to lose a boy just because I took eternity to get ready and to build up the courage to talk to him.* He deserved to know how I really felt. Everyone deserves to know if someone loves them back.

"He's right over there," Grace said, elbowing me and pointing toward our right.

"Where?"

"Right there." Grace repeated, grabbing my face and pointing it directly to where Liam was sitting. "Don't you see him?" She let go of my head and stood facing me, her arms crossed over her chest.

"Yes." I said, out of breath at the sight of his handsome form in that, tight black suit. "I see him."

Whatever I do next is going to change my life in so many drastic ways. But will it be for better or worse? I'll never know if I don't give Liam and me a chance. It would be my first-time experiencing love other than sisterly love, which I was well familiar with. All through our childhood, I had cared for Winter and looked after her as well. I drove her to dates and gave her advice I thought she would take. Back then, I didn't know how immature she was. *I will never understand how she can throw away such a*

166

beautiful thing as love. True, I was definitely not an expert at it. I had never been in love and meeting Liam was the first time I had been truly open to it. I may have been new at love, but careless I was not. I wouldn't be able to live with myself if I was ever the reason that someone lost all hope for finding love.

"Go!" Grace gave me a little push toward where Liam was sitting.

Even though he didn't have his eyes glued to his phone I was not surprised that he hadn't spotted me. Instead, he was looking down at the table with his face in his hands. Even at that angle, I could see the sadness and disappointment in his eyes and facial expression. Again I felt awful for making him wait for hours. I wanted to know what he was thinking. I wanted to banish all of his worries and insecurities about me and about us. *I don't want him to think for another second that I don't love him because I truly do.*

He must have been deep in thought since I was literally standing right behind him, and he hadn't noticed.

167

WHY NOT SOMEONE ELSE?

What should I say first? I don't want to let my nervousness show. Maybe I don't have to say anything. If I grab one of those metal chairs, pull it next to him, and sit down; Liam might start the conversation instead. What if I just say 'hi'? I wondered. *But won't that startle him? Gosh, why do I have to always overthink everything? I shouldn't feel anxious to talk to someone I love.* The problem was that everything Winter told me was in the back of my head, messing with my happy thoughts.

"Summer," Liam turned around quickly and stared into my eyes. He looked surprised, relieved, happy, and excited — all at once. "You came." He gave me a proud and comforting smile which I, of course, returned.

I never understood how Winter could be so carefree, happy, and spontaneous when I always felt as if I needed to be in hiding. No matter how small and insignificant something might be, my mind would always make a huge deal out of it. However, seeing Liam smiling like that because of me, made all of that night's worries seem so pathetic.

How did I ever think about not giving us a chance? We are basically the perfect match.

"I thought you weren't going to show up." Liam stood up, moved his chair closer to the table, and backed up a small step to be closer to where I was standing, leaving barely any space between our bodies.

"I know. I'm really late. I am so sorry," I said as I stood stiffly mere inches from his body.

"I don't care, Summer. I'm just happy that you're here." Liam took a small step closer to me, causing our bodies to slightly brush against one another. "You look lovely," he said, reaching for my hands.

"Thank you. You don't look bad either." I held on to his cold hands as we stared into each other's eyes.

Our faces only an inch apart, I could feel his breath on my lips and imagined that he felt mine as well. I could see the pores of his skin and every little detail of his beautiful, unique green eyes. How was it that vibrant green eyes could also have dark blue intertwined in them

— as if the ocean had met up with a valley full of dark green grass? All this time, I'd thought his eyes the most delightful green I'd ever seen. What I hadn't been close enough to discern before was their special and unique blend of shades of green and almost a navy blue. *He is probably the only guy in the world with this peculiar eye color. But it who he is. Liam is such a peculiar guy. Maybe that's the thing I adore most about him.* I'd never been interested in someone ordinary. I wanted someone with their own unique personality traits. I wanted someone who was not moving along with the crowd but instead setting his own path. For me, Liam was all of those things and more. He was not just like everyone else. *He is the one I have chosen to open up to and love. He is the lucky guy who finally locked my heart with his.*

"Liam, you were right about everything," I said, breaking the silence between us.

"What part? You know I said a lot yesterday." He let go of my hands so he could stroke my blushing cheek.

170

"You know what I meant. You always do." I placed my hand on top of his and began to tilt my head.

I closed my eyes the moment I felt the warmth steaming from his palm. *I could do this all day. I like how slow his movements are. I love the way he is speaking so gently but still loud enough for me to hear it over that annoying music. If only we could stay like this forever!*

"I want you to say it." He stopped holding my cheek to place his index finger under my chin and lift up my head.

Our faces were getting closer and closer by the second. He may have said he wanted me to talk, but his lips were telling my mouth otherwise. I had never kissed anyone. *Am I about to experience fireworks the second his lips touch mine?*

"I love —" Suddenly my trance of earnest words gurgled to a stop by the freezing water that was hitting my face.

"What is your issue?" Liam screamed at Winter in anger and frustration. As for me, I wasn't surprised. I'd already imagined

171

something like that happening from someone as immature and selfish as Winter.

"How about *she* tells you what my issue is?" Winter yelled back, throwing the water bottle at me.

"I am *not* doing this," I said. "Not tonight." I turned to walk away from the scene caused by my maniac sister.

"Where do you think you're going?" Winter yelled, grabbing my arm tightly to drag me back to within inches of her face.

"I am going home. Just so you know, you are making a fool of yourself," I told her with an assertive tone.

Everyone left in the gym — teachers, students, and who-knows-who-else were all listening to everything and staring with dead eyes. *How embarrassing can this get?*

"Fine. Let's go outside." Winter let go of my arm and rushed out of the gym, slamming everything and everyone out of her way.

I'd never seen her that angry in public. She would never let strangers see her vulnerability. *Clearly, tonight is different. There's no running away. I chose this. Now, it is time to face it.*

"I am coming with you." Liam appeared behind me and gave me a reassuring pat on the shoulder.

"Thank you."

He doesn't need to be here to see this blow up between us. He's not the problem. If he stays with us the whole time, Winter may try to blame everything on him. On the other hand, I was filled with such anger, fear, and frustration at the thought of being left alone in that sisterly battle. I needed him by my side. *After all, he is why I'm doing all of this.* I needed to be reassured that my choice was worth it. *If my suspicions are right about who Winter really is, she is going to bring me down in every way possible. I really can't let that happen. I can't let her get away with this, and I won't.*

The moment I opened the doors, I felt my heart drop all the way to my stomach. *Winter might be younger than me, but when she gets extremely angry, she can be the most intimidating person around.*

"What? Are you going to go home and tell mom that I splashed water all over you? Just wait 'til she finds out what you are doing!" I could tell that Winter was revving up to say things designed to scare me off. "I am so stupid to believe that you cared about me. Like why would I even think about that? It's not like you even cared to hang out with me or talk to me for the past two years. You know, they were my parents too, Summer. You weren't the only one who felt mad and sad about dad and mom getting a divorce. But no, of course you would shut yourself off. Of course, you wouldn't talk to your little sister about it. You know what? Screw you!"

During a seeming pause in yelling at me, she stared at me blankly — as if for a response. That I didn't say anything or show any emotion made her furious to the point that she rushed toward me and grabbed for my hair.

"Don't you dare!" Liam said, blocking her hand and pushing her away from us. "What is your problem?"

"Really?" Winter began to laugh hysterically.

174

Liam and I looked at each other in fear and confusion. Not knowing what to do, we just waited for her to finally be done with whatever she was doing.

"I begged you for another chance, and instead, you ghosted me," Winter said in a loud, raspy voice. "Then, I see you about to kiss my sister, and you have the audacity to ask me what is wrong with *me*?" Her face had turned so red that she seemed to be wearing no makeup at all. Her face was shiny with tears and her hair all frizzy and messed up.

"You cheated on me!" Liam shot back "What? Did you really think that you being sorry was going to fix it all? Things don't work that way, Winter. I stopped liking you the moment I saw you kissing that dude. No amount of spamming my phone was going to fix that."

"But I love you!" Winter said, as if saying that would be enough to erase all the bad and make him remember the few good moments they'd had together. Maybe that would cause him to change his mind and choose her.

"I don't love you anymore, Winter. I haven't loved you for months." Liam looked back at my sorrowful face. "Why can't you just accept the fact that I love your sister? Just let her be happy."

A cacophony of emotions were bombarding my mind. I felt sorry for everything that was going on. I wanted to hug Winter and let her know that Liam was not going to be the only guy she would ever be in love with, that someone was out there waiting for her. *Why can't she let him go and just find someone who can love her?*

"Summer doesn't deserve to be happy. She is a liar and a traitor." Winter exclaimed and went for my hair again. And again, Liam stopped her before she could get any closer to me.

"How can you say that?" I asked. "I have done nothing but care for you and your happiness your whole life, Winter, and you know that."

"If you cared about my happiness, you wouldn't be trying to get the guy I still love." Winter struggled to get away from Liam who was gripping her arms.

"Winter, if you had told me that Liam was the guy we saw in the store, I would have stayed away from him. You were the one who lied. I asked you who he was because I found him attractive. How was I supposed to know you dated him when you didn't even tell me the name of the guy you dated during summer camp? Am I a psychic? But you are right. I should have stayed away from him after you told me who he was, but Winter, you never gave me the chance to tell you how I really felt. You commanded me to stay away after I was already completely in love with him. At that point, the only thing keeping me away from him was my loyalty to you," I said, pausing to catch my breath.

"Don't make me laugh, Summer," Winter looked back in disbelief and then took a step closer to ensure that she'd be in my face. "I guess your loyalty to me didn't last that long since you are here doing exactly what you promised you wouldn't do."

"How dare you give me a lecture about loyalty when clearly you don't know what it means. You think I was never going to find out about everything that you have been doing and all of the guys you've been hooking up with since school started? Now I know that you have never been sincere with your feelings. You might say that you still love Liam, but your actions say otherwise. Nothing you can say could convince me that I'm wrong. I have proof, Winter. I know you don't love him, so give it up."

"Fine, but don't you dare talk to me again. From today on, you mean nothing to me." Winter yanked the keys from my purse and launched herself toward the half-empty parking lot.

"Fine, I cannot wait to talk to you later." I yelled before Winter got in her car.

She slammed the car's door so hard that I expected to see the car window shatter. Winter's car surged recklessly across and then out of the school parking lot, the car radio blaring. *Oh my goodness, I hope she gets home safely. How could I ever forgive myself if something happened to her?* I might have been mad at her, but I still cared about her. *I will always love her. At the end of the day, she is my sister. We are going to have each other for the rest of our lives — whether she likes it or not.*

Chapter 10

It seemed like eons had passed while I stared at the empty parking spot. Winter had driven away so carelessly and fast that five seconds after her right foot had touched the gas, her car was no longer in sight. I was left to wonder what I should do. *Should I call my mom and tell her what happened? Should I warn her about Winter's fragile state? Should I just go home instead of being with Liam?* I had no clue about what to do. My mind was telling me to run home as fast as I could, but my heart was telling me to stay there with Liam. I had gotten dressed up and put on makeup to do one thing and still hadn't done it. *I have to let Liam know how I really feel. Oh . . . Liam!* I'd totally forgotten that Liam had been standing behind me that whole time. I hadn't even thanked him for

180

blocking my sister — twice. It was bad enough that I'd put him in the middle of such a messy situation in the first place. I just hoped he could forget about it all because I certainly wished I could.

I turn around slowly to get a glimpse of him. He was not as close to me as I thought he would be. Apparently at some point he had begun to put some space between us. *He is probably trying to give me time to think. Surely, he knows why I'm here. So, why is he insisting that I say it? Are the words so important to him? Is he going to feel satisfaction from my confession of love toward him?* I just hoped it wouldn't scare him away. I had no clue what I was doing. I'd never gone on a date, never held hands with a boy, never been kissed, never lain with someone…

"It's okay if you want to go after her. She's your sister. I know you're worried about her." Liam turned away and began walking toward a nearby bench.

"I don't have a car anymore." I looked down at my feet and suddenly registered how tremendously they were hurting from those high heels. *Girls who go around wearing heels just for fun — do they really not feel any pain or do they just get used to it?*

Slowly and deliberately, I began to walk toward him. Every step echoed across the empty parking lot. I hadn't realized until just then that we were the only souls left there.

"Right… I see. Do you want me to give you a ride, then?" As Liam looked me up and down, he suddenly gave a start when his eyes got to those stupid heels.

"Yes, if you don't mind. I don't want my mom to have to deal with Winter by herself this late at night, but mom's the only one who can keep my sister from doing something stupid." I sat down next to him and began to remove the heels. In addition to the red marks all over them, my pinkie was blistered and the skin on the bottoms of my feet was peeling off. *How gross can this get?*

"That looks kinda painful. Here, let me grab your heels," Liam said, snatching up my shoes before I even had time to respond. After jumping up from the bench, he began to place one arm behind my back and the other behind my legs. One moment, I had been peacefully sitting on the bench, and the next, I was being lifted in the air by Liam Carter.

"What are you doing?" I gasped, tightly holding on to him. I'd never thought of him as being particularly strong. But in this case, all I could think of was how attractive he seemed. I could feel his muscles and his bones. I could see the texture of his hair and feel the warmth of his neck.

"With all the pain you're in, did you think I was going let you walk another step in those stupid heels." Liam walked steadily across the parking lot with me in his arms.

"Thank you, but you really didn't have to carry me. Just getting those shoes off was heavenly." He stopped walking.

"And let you walk barefoot? Not on my watch." He looked straight into my dark brown eyes and then away when our faces almost touched. A second after we broke eye contact, he cleared his throat and slowly lowered me to my feet.

"Thank you," I said, quickly adjusting the side slit in my dress and grabbing my shoes from him. Somehow that dress had become tighter on my body with every breath I'd taken over the past two hours. *Is that a good thing or a bad thing? It's not as if Liam already saw my bloody feet just a few minutes ago.*

Without saying a word, Liam opened my door and then began slowly walking to the other side of the car. After everything that had happened, I still hadn't mustered enough courage to tell him how I felt. No matter how much Liam clearly wanted me to declare my feelings, I knew myself to be a coward who just kept talking about everything except for what's really important. *I can't keep doing this. It's so selfish of me to keep him wondering. He deserves so much better.*

At that point, I didn't know exactly what real love is, but I did know what it isn't. Love shouldn't be filled with lies and betrayals or arguments and jealousy. Instead, it should be full of compassion and devotion to one another. Love can be beautiful when both people are determined to choose each other over and over no matter what happens and no matter how many years have gone by. It can thrive only when the purest of hearts meet and are happily joined together. *But what does Liam think about what his love for me should be?* Two different-minded people can never love each other until death. Their differences would eventually cause them to drift apart.

If I don't admit to him that I love him, all the time I spent gaining the courage to stand up to Winter has gone to waste. Why on earth am I so scared to do this? Am I just too embarrassed to let myself be vulnerable with someone I met only two months ago? After all, I had risked my relationship with my sister for a relationship I was not sure of. *What if Liam and I start dating and then find out that we're not right for each other? What if all this love turns into hatred? What if at the end of the day I end up all alone again? On the other hand, if I let all of this be for nothing; I will be too ashamed to ever again face myself in the mirror.*

"Aren't you going to get in?" Liam called, still standing outside the driver's side of the car with the door wide open.

I don't know. Am I? What kind of person would I be to just sit quietly the whole ride home?

185

"Liam," I said, trying to still my trembling body.

The quiet friendship we had slowly developed would not be the same, but I had to tell him how I felt so I could learn how he felt in return. *Things will never begin unless I open up the door to the possibility of us being together.* I smiled with satisfaction at the thought of us together.

"Are you okay? What's wrong?" Liam hadn't left the side of the car. He stood waiting for an answer, but I could see him starting to get a little bit worried that I might collapse the way I almost did the day of the first pep rally at the football stadium.

"I love you," I whispered.

It had become so cold that I could see my foggy breath in front of me. I knew he couldn't hear me, that I needed to say it louder, but I was so afraid. The whole time, I had been solely focusing on what could go wrong and completely ignoring all the things that could go right. *I love Liam. I have loved him since my first glimpse of him. To be with this guy, I am willing to risk it all.*

"I'm sorry. I can't hear what you're saying," he said, staring straight at me from over the top of the car.

In the moment his words had taken, the powerful and unknown feelings roiling inside of me had begun to take control. I had a huge urge to scream his name out loud. I wanted the universe to know how I felt. *This is my chance! This is my moment!*

"I love you!" I yelled, the words filled with power and fervor.

"I love you, Liam," I repeated more tenderly.

Liam stared blankly at me, his face unreadable. *Is he happy or sad? Surprised or annoyed? Why doesn't he say something?*

"You love me?" Liam said — finally. Without closing the car door, he began walking toward me.

His face beamed with contentment, crowned by the purest smile I had ever seen. *Nothing could ever make me regret this moment.*

"Summer," Liam said, cupping my face in his cold hands.

"Yeah?" I said, surprised to find my gaze so effortless.

187

"I love you." Liam pulled my face closer to his and began to gently place a kiss on my lips. Just then, he pulled away for a second to look back into my eyes. *He is waiting for permission. He doesn't want to overstep. Even though he clearly wants me more than ever, he still cares enough to make sure I am comfortable around him.* "I love you, Summer."

"I love you too, Liam."

This time we both leaned in for a kiss — our freezing, red noses just touching. His warm and wonderfully soft lips pressed against mine gently and slowly, as if he wanted to cherish every second of it. So intent were we to explore each other's mouths, we might have been kissing for seconds or even hours.

Who knows? This moment is all I ever dreamed of. We slowly pulled away. A cold breeze suddenly came out of nowhere, and the red and orange leaves flew all around us. As we turned to take it all in, we began to laugh. It wasn't the kind of chuckle at something funny. It was more like the laughter that escapes when you are overwhelmed with joy.

I began to dance in circles with my arms spread out around me. The breeze helped my hair stay off my back while my dress flowed effortlessly as I continued to move. Liam just looked at me, but his look was one I hadn't ever been personally familiar with. He was looking at me with love — as if I was the most precious gift he had ever received. *Do I really make him feel this way, or is it all in my head?*

"You are so beautiful." Liam walked toward me, extending his right hand for me to take. "May I have this dance?" He bowed a little, making sure to keep his eyes on me.

"You certainly may," I said and elegantly placed my right hand on his.

He pulled me closer as we began to slow dance in the empty parking lot in the middle of the night. The sky was overflowing with sparkling stars and the moon full and bright. He spun me once and twice, and after each one pulled me closer to him. We were dancing like people used to in the old days. This is the first time I had ever danced with someone, so I was surprised to be doing a fairly decent job of it.

Probably it was because we were doing only simple movements — take one step to the front and then one step to the back. After every step and every spin, our gazes always ended up reconnecting. On the last spin, he tightly held on to me. As he embraced me, I heard a single sob. I couldn't tell if he was crying from sadness or happiness. Maybe it was both.

"What's wrong?" I whispered in his ear and began to run my hand up and down his back in an effort to comfort him.

"It's stupid," he whispered back. He began to mirror my hands' motions but on my bare back.

"What you are feeling is never stupid. I want to know. Tell me."

I stopped rubbing and rested my hand on his lower back.

"I'm just so happy that I met you," Liam whispered in my ear while pressing me to him. "You might think I am weird, but I always wanted to meet someone who looked at me with the same purity that she saw in my face. I wanted to see the love in her eyes and not just

190

hear it from her lips. I have always wanted to hear it, see it, feel it —
experience all of it for myself. The moment my eyes fell on you, I
longed to cherish you. I wanted to get to know the real you but feared
that it was forbidden to me because I'd dated your sister.

"I guess she did love me but not in the way I've always hoped
for. I don't know how to explain it. I sensed something holding her
back. She couldn't love me in that way, and she is never going to. I let
go of all of my love for her so that I could someday give it to someone
who actually deserved it, someone I knew would give me the same love
back. Call it old school, but that is who I am. I knew you liked me back
because you attempted to stay away from me. All those days you tried
to ignore me, I knew what you were doing, and I admired you for that
— at least at the beginning.

"However, it was making me so mad to see your sister treating
you as if you meant nothing to her. I wanted for you to let me in, even
if just as a friend. Something was telling me to be patient to let you
figure things out on your own. I was not going to risk things by making

191

things go a little bit faster, no matter how much I wanted them to. All the time I spent away, watching from a distance, was worth it — to make my heart right for you.

"Summer, I cannot guarantee that I won't ever hurt you or disappoint you. We are both young and soon will be leaving for college. But I want to assure you of one thing: As long as you let me, I will love you entirely with my whole being. Each and every day we spend together I will cherish you. When you struggle, I will be there to help and comfort you and to wipe away all of your tears. I will never make plans that will take me away from you for too long. I will put our relationship above my career.

"I will become a better person for you. I will be the best doctor you will ever meet so that I can take care of you when you're sick. I will hold you and never let you go. My eyes will never wander from yours. I will protect your heart as if it is my greatest treasure — because it truly is. I will respect your body and soul with gentleness. I will go wherever you want to go. I will help you build your dreams and accomplish all of your wishes. All I want is to be with you, Summer. All I have ever wanted these past two months is to hold you in my arms and share this love with you," Liam sighed heavily. "I know it's a lot. I have never said this much without stopping before." He paused to press his forehead against mine with his eyes completely shut. Then he went on.

"I didn't mean to overwhelm you, but somehow I know that you think the same about me." Liam opened his eyes wide and leaned over for a gentle kiss. "You can call me weird if you want to." He pulled away, giving me a tragic look of embarrassment.

"I don't think you're weird." I gave him another kiss and lingered close to his lips for a second before speaking. "I'm not going to lie, though. When you said it aloud, it sounded kind of cheesy." I poked his nose with my index finger and then turned to make my escape.

"Cheesy, huh?" he said, chasing after me and catching me in a matter of seconds. "Did you think you were going to get very far barefooted?" he said, hugging me from behind. I felt his warm body against mine.

"I may have forgotten about that." I looked down at my disgusting feet which had started bleeding from several places from the small rocks I'd stepped on while trying to run away.

"Here we go again," Liam said, swooping me up to carry me back to his car. But unlike before, he placed me on the passenger seat, kissed me on the forehead, and made his way over to his side.

"What do you think is going to happen when I get home?" I asked as soon as he'd turned on the car and blasted the heater all the way.

"Who knows? Maybe your mom got a chance to talk some sense into her. If you want, call me right when you get into your bedroom," Liam said with a glance over at me along with his signature smile, "and we can talk all night."

"Sure, why not." We exchanged phones quietly and awkwardly as we typed each other's contact information.

On the drive to my house, it was all I could to stop sighing with deep satisfaction every few minutes. All those weeks, I had been trying to deny how I felt, to hide and stay silent as I watched everyone else move on with their lives. I avoided being with people, especially boys. In an effort to forget about Liam, I'd pretended to not feel anything for him at all. But no matter how hard I tried, nothing worked. All that time, I kept wondering why I was so attached to a guy I'd known for such a short time. Yet somehow, I had sensed that ours could be the purest kind of love any two people can ever share at such a young age. The more I thought about everything he'd told me that night, the more certain I was. Yes, I thought with another sigh, that is what we have. Finally, we are together.

*　　*　　*　　*　　*　　*

"Promise you will call me tonight if you get bored," Liam said as he carried me to the front door of my house. I had my heels and purse in my right hand while my left arm was clinging to him.

"I promise," I said as I looked at him effortlessly, a gentle smile on my face.

Once we were a few inches from the door, Liam put me down. Then, as soon as I put my burdens down, I stretched my hands behind his neck and reached up for a quick kiss. As I'd hoped, the peck turned into a long, passionate kiss.

Even though I'd never felt so content, I knew I'd finally have to let him go. It was getting late, and I still didn't have a clue about how far he had to drive to get home. Plus, I could sense in my bones that someone was anticipating my arrival. *I wouldn't be surprised if right now she's watching from one of the windows.*

"I really don't want you to leave, but I have to talk to my sister. I owe her at least that much," I said, reluctantly moving away from him.

"You're right. Are you going to call me before you go to bed?" Liam held both of my hands, clutching them against his chest and warm coat.

"I will, but I'm not sure how late it will be. Just send me a text when you get home so I'll know you arrived in one piece." I gave him a quick final kiss on his pale cheek.

"I will." Liam lifted my right hand to his mouth and planted a kiss on it. "I love you, Summer."

"I love you, Liam," I said, my words catching him just as he turned to walk toward his car.

I didn't move from that spot on the porch until I'd seen him drive off and his car disappear from sight. Already this had been one of the most eventful nights of my life, and it wasn't over yet. *I can feel Winter waiting for me on the other side of this door. Is she going to be pissed and try to hit me? Or what if I'm just overreacting? Maybe she's had time to calm down a little and reflect on things. She could be waiting there to ask me questions about my night. I'll never know until I open this door. It's not like I can stay on the porch for the rest of the night. It's freezing out here!*

197

Chapter 11

Why am I worrying? Winter said she never wanted to talk to me again. She's probably in her room crying, or maybe, she's already asleep by now. I could see that my mom had already gone to bed. I wasn't surprised — since she had to go to work early the next morning. Once again, Winter and I would be home all alone all weekend. Yet, this time it was probably for the best. *It might be the only chance I'll ever get to mend my relationship with Winter. I'm going to have to talk to her sooner or later.*

Our rooms were next to each other; we shared a bathroom, ate dinner together, and shared a car as well. *No way Winter can hold onto a grudge against me for long. It is not like I'm going to college far away either.* I expected her to move away as far as possible the moment she got the chance — but not for years. *I wouldn't be surprised if she decides to get a plane ticket to move in with our dad. After all, she is still daddy's little girl.*

After locking the front door behind me, I walked down the hall. No matter how lightly I stepped, with my every footfall, the noise made by the wooden floorboards echoed throughout the house. I hated it. I was going to end up waking up everybody. At that point, I was too tired to deal with Winter and besides that had no clue what to say.

As soon as I opened my door, my heart dropped down to my stomach. I could feel a knot beginning to form in my throat the moment my eyes fell on Winter who was sitting patiently on my bed. She didn't look mad, but she didn't look happy, either. Her eyes were red and puffy, and her nose sounded congested as she took quiet breaths.

"How was your night?" Winter began as she slid over to make room for me to sit on the bed.

"It was okay." I turned around to start placing my purse on top of my chest of drawers and my shoes on the floor.

"Do you love him?" She asked while I was still turned away from her.

"You know I do," I said, still in the same position and still looking at my heels on the floor. *Why is she here in the first place? I thought she didn't want to talk to me.*

"So, are you guys a thing now?" Winter asked, her voice starting to sound irritated. Clearly, she was still hurt by my actions.

"Why are you doing this?" I sat down on the floor right next to my door and waited for Winter to respond. She looked at me as if I'd just said the meanest insult in the world.

"Well, I'm just so sorry for trying to be a good sister and wanting to know how your lovely night went with *my* boyfriend," Winter said, raising her voice with the last words. "Sorry, I meant to say *ex*-boyfriend," she said, then placed her right hand over her mouth.

"It's fine." I stood up. Even though I walked over to sit next to her on my bed, I continued to focus my eyes on the floor. My body was bristling with the sense of friction between us. I couldn't remember the last time we'd had an argument. And whenever that was, it certainly wasn't over a boy.

"Whatever... It's not your fault," Winter said as she grabbed my left arm and placed her head on my shoulder.

I was still on my guard, scared that she was going to lash out. *I know how bad she's hurting so why is she lying to me? Is she trying to hide how mad she still is as part of a plan to get back at me?*

"Summer," Winter spoke softly, her head still resting on my shoulder.

"Yeah?" I tried to turn my face a little to look at her, but all I could see was the top of her head.

"Will you promise me one thing?" Winter lifted up her head from my shoulder to look me straight in the eye.

"What is it?" I tilted my head and readjusted my position so my whole body was facing hers.

"Promise me you won't cheat on Liam like I did." Winter held out her pinkie in front of her.

201

"I promise." I offered mine, and we sealed the promise.

"Also… I am really sorry for how I reacted outside the gym. It was not fair to you. I was the one who messed things up for good." Winter took a deep breath and stared at me for a beat. "You didn't deserve to get your hair and makeup ruined with the water I splashed on you," she added and began to move my hair out of my face. "I'm sorry. I was being a bit immature. It won't happen again. I promise."

"It's fine," I cut in, beginning to reach out to her slowly in an attempt to give her a hug. Midway, she stopped me.

"Let me finish." She reached out to hold me away from her. "Last summer, I found out that Dad cheated on Mom," she said, pausing to turn toward me. "When I confronted him about it, he said that you already knew about everything." Again, Winter paused, as if searching for the right words. "I just want to know one thing. Why didn't you tell me? Were you really going to just let me go on with my life without knowing the truth about the divorce? Do you really think I

202

am that stupid?" With the last words, her tone escalated from soft spoken to angry.

"Mom and Dad begged me not to tell you, Winter." I moved closer and placed my hand on top of her arm to comfort her, but Winter pulled away from me.

"I don't care. You should have told me anyways instead of lying to me about it for years," she screamed as a tear splashed from her left eye and her face reddened in anger.

"I know!" I yelled back, clasping my hands on top of my head. "I know," I said again, but gently. "I am sorry."

A few minutes of silence went by. Winter began to sob quietly while I sat motionless next to her, trying to keep from upsetting her even more.

"I hate you," Winter whispered underneath her breath.

"Why?" I stared at her with sympathy even though it seemed she couldn't care less about anything I might have been feeling at that point.

203

"Because you let me believe Mom was the bad guy for asking Dad for a divorce. Why would you do that?" She stood up from the bed and began to pace around the room.

"I never wanted you to believe Mom was the villain, but I also knew how much you love Dad. I didn't want to take that away from you."

"You don't get to choose for me, Summer," Winter yelled, turning around to confront me from across the room.

"I know that, Winter. I was just trying to protect you." I stood up and began to walk toward her.

"I didn't need you to protect me." She pushed me away harshly, causing me to fall back on the bed.

"Gosh, I'm sorry! What else do you want me to say?" I stood back up, this time keeping my distance from her.

"I don't know," Winter moaned and slowly began to sob.

She looks so lost and angry — probably how I looked when I found Dad with the other woman. *She wants someone to blame. Sadly, I'm the one she's chosen.*

"Is everything okay?" Mom asked from the doorway.

As one, Winter and I looked at Mom, who seemed barely awake. I felt so bad for her. For the past two years her life had been hell. The last thing she needed was for her daughters to start hating each other.

"Everything's fine," Winter said, standing up to walk toward the doorway.

"Where do you think you're going?" Mom moved to block her way out of the room.

"I'm going back to my room," Winter said, attempting to go around our mother.

"No, you are not. You can go back to your room after I am done talking to you both." Mom pushed Winter completely inside my room and slammed the door behind her.

After that, Winter gave up and walked back to sit next to me, all the way sending me an annoyed look. Winter might have been pissed at mom, but at that point, I was fearing for both our lives.

"Can someone explain to me what's going on?" Mom grabbed the chair from my study desk and placed it a few inches away from us.

Winter and I just looked at her intently as if she was an intruder.

"So, now neither of you want to talk?" Mom said, with growing anger. "Summer, how was your night? Were you able to talk to the guy you told me about?"

I stared at her in wide-eyed shock at the questions she'd just asked me — and right in front of Winter. *Does she want Winter to murder both of us tonight, or what?*

"Really, mom? You're asking Summer about how her night went with my ex-boyfriend?" Winter said, looking both baffled and mad.

"Winter, let me ask you this. Why are you so angry at your sister when you have clearly moved on? Last I checked, you've already been dating multiple other guys. Am I not correct?" Mom had shifted her focus from me to my sister.

Mom was planning something, but I hadn't yet figured out what it was.

"But mom! I still love Liam!" Winter yelled and began to cry.

"Winter, what do you love about him?" Mom asked, and I marveled at her ability to keep her tone so calm and passive while being screamed at in the middle of the night by her own daughter. *I bet she wants to slap her.*

Winter's face reflected a slowly changing parade of expressions from numbness to confusion to dawning realization. *Has Winter finally figured out that she is not in love with Liam anymore?*

"I don't know." Winter continued to cry, but her tone seemed to have moved from out-and-out grief to mere frustration.

"What do you mean you don't know, sweetie?" Mom leaned forward to reach for Winter's hand.

"I mean I don't know, Mom," Winter said, slapping Mom's hand out of the way. "Did you know if Dad really loved you?"

"So, that's what all this is about." Mom sighed.

"What do you mean? It was always about that. I finally found someone who loves me, and then I have to find out about the most horrible thing ever. Is it fair that all of you betrayed me, and I ended up making stupid choices that I've regretted every second of my life? I love Liam, Mom. Why can't anyone understand that? Do you just want me to pretend that I'm okay with her dating him? If so, you're out of your mind! I would rather die than have to see them together."

"Okay, Winter." I said, frustrated. "I just don't understand it. If you claim to love him, then why are you going around kissing every guy who comes your way?"

When is she going to understand that what she feels isn't real? *How long can a person be in denial? This new Winter is the kind of girl who moves on quickly from one boy to the next without looking back.* Why couldn't she let go of Liam?

Winter stared at me in silence. *Could it be that she doesn't know the answer either? What does she think love looks like?* I wondered. *She doesn't seem to have a clue.*

"It's just not fair. I was happy, made one little mistake, and then lost everything because of it. I lost Liam. I lost you. I lost Dad. And I hate you, Mom, for not telling me the truth. I was so happy and now, I feel depressed all the time. For once, you have everything, Summer, while I have nothing. That's so weird to me, and it's unfair." Winter hugged her legs to her chest and rested her head face-down on her arms.

"Darling, I'm sorry I didn't tell you about your dad, but after I saw how much it hurt your sister, I didn't want you to go through the same thing." Mom sat next to Winter on the bed.

"But Dad hurt you, Mom, and all this time I've been talking to him like nothing happened. He freakin' cheated on you!"

209

Winter turned around to face me with an offended look. "Is that why you never call him, and he doesn't give you any money?"

"Yeah. Did you think I was going to take his money after everything he did?" I asked.

"Hey, I still would have taken his money as a way for him to pay for his mistake. You have to be smarter, Summer. You're not going to have your little sister around to figure things out for you much longer. Once I graduate, I will be long gone out of this small, boring town."

"Young lady, this boring town has given you a lot of memories and friends," Mom said defensively.

"As if I couldn't make them in a different place," Winter murmured.

Mom elbowed Winter and pinned her down on the bed. At that point they were both lying down while I was still sitting next to Winter and facing toward mom and her.

"Get over here. I want to tell you something." Mom signaled me to lie down next to Winter.

Once beside Winter, I looked up to the white ceiling. The room was so quiet that we could hear the bugs outside my window trying to get in. I felt so exhausted. I had never so longed for a shower in my whole life. I imagined lying there alone, all clean and snuggly on my bed and talking to Liam on the other side of the phone. Actually, I wished he was there physically, but knew it was too soon for that. *Is just being able to talk to him too much to ask?* I couldn't push my sister and my mom out of my room — especially since it seemed as if we were making some real progress. I was almost confident enough to think that Winter wouldn't be dreaming about all the ways she could end my relationship with Liam.

"So, how was your night?" Mom asked from across the bed, her head tilted toward Winter's.

"Mine was boring, but I bet Summer got her first kiss," Winter broke in. *I guess she's trying to reassure me that we are okay again by teasing me about how pathetic I am.*

"Wait, what?" Mom sounded both surprised and overjoyed. "Is it true?"

With my gaze still on the ceiling, I covered the side of my face so that they couldn't see how much I was blushing. What can I say? My first kiss was with Liam Carter — in the middle of a windy and chilly autumn night under a sky full of shining stars. It may have been awkward, but it was also gentle and perfect. My first kiss wasn't what anyone would call passionate or even sexual. Liam certainly didn't make me feel used or uncomfortable either.

At that exact moment, I had been in the safest place I could ever be — in my boyfriend's arms. I shared my first kiss with the one I loved first, and the one I fell head over heels for. I couldn't have asked for a better moment than that. *Of one thing I am certain: I plan to give myself*

212

completely and love this person more than anyone else in the world. I am sure he is going to wholeheartedly love me back.

THE END

About the author

Isangelic Reyes is currently seeking a degree in English Education in hopes of becoming a professor. Her current residency is in South Alabama, but her heart longs to live in Florida. Born in Puerto Rico, Reyes is fluent in Spanish and seeks to make her family proud with her very first self-published novel— *Why Not Someone Else?*